CITY
wolves

Previous Books by Mike Chase

Beyond Remorse

Spotlight on History

CITY
wolves

— A Novel —

BY: MIKE CHASE

iUniverse, Inc.
Bloomington

City Wolves

iUniverse books may be ordered through booksellers or by contacting:

iUniverse
1663 Liberty Drive
Bloomington, IN 47403
www.iuniverse.com
1-800-Authors (1-800-288-4677)

ISBN: 978-1-4759-6370-0 (sc)
ISBN: 978-1-4759-6372-4 (hc)
ISBN: 978-1-4759-6371-7 (ebk)

Library of Congress Control Number: 2012922416

Printed in the United States of America

iUniverse rev. date: 12/13/2012

For Anna

Chapter One

He was slightly less than six feet tall, with a fleshy, prominent nose, dark hair, thick mustache, and fierce black eyes. His teeth were broken in the front and badly stained from tobacco. He had long, powerful arms and walked with the quiet, graceful movements of a cat. He was a quiet man . . . almost aloof. He spoke with a soft tone when with strangers; even among his friends, he was decidedly reserved. He had a cavalier way with women, whether they were common whores or ladies who lifted their skirts aside when he passed. Most of his female companions thought that he was a gentleman through and through. He dressed in fine silk suits cut with an Italian flair.

His name was Vincentiso Gargotta. He carried a six-shot blue steel .38 caliber revolver in his waistband, and he was a deadly shot. He was also a con man, burglar, extortionist, murderer, and an enforcer for the Kansas City mob. He had traveled extensively throughout the United States doing various jobs for the organization. Although most people considered him a gentleman, he was deadly when the blood lust was upon him. It seemed that the blood lusts were constantly upon him lately. He had a criminal dossier with Kansas City and other law enforcement agencies which listed twenty men he was known to have killed. He had killed them all in cold blood and had never been prosecuted.

Gargotta preferred working alone when doing the mob's business. In some cases he used three close friends who were from the old country. He was born in Sicily in the town of Castillammare del Golfo in 1895. Castillammare del Golfo is situated deep inside an emerald gulf at the western tip of Sicily. The name means "castle by the sea". There is an ancient castle in the center of the town's waterfront. The wind, when it blows hot and dusty across the sea from the Libyan Desert, carries the aroma of fresh grapefruits and lemons.

Gargotta spent his first twenty years in this town, working the fields along with his father and brothers. His father was a soldier in the mafia, which was run by the Buccellatos family. Throughout the early years of Vincentiso's childhood, his father excelled in Mafioso activities and became a respected man. His fortune increased, and he became a landowner who raised cattle and horses.

Vincentiso's mother encouraged him to finish high school and to prepare for college. However, by the time he was eighteen, his father had influenced him to become a member of the Sicilian Mafia. He had killed his first man before reaching his nineteenth birthday. Vincentiso was now riding high in the society of criminals.

At the outbreak of World War I in 1915, Vincentiso was drafted into the Italian Army and assigned to the artillery unit. His regiment was sent to the Austrian border, in the thick of the fighting. In one battle, almost all the men in the regiment were wiped out. Vincentiso, one of the few survivors, was badly wounded and captured by the German Army. While in captivity, he realized that co-operating with the Germans made his captivity and recuperation that much easier.

The Germans found that Vincentiso picked up the German language very easily and was extremely intelligent. Before the end of the war, Vincentiso became both a collaborator and spy and was sent home. Once at home, he realized that if he stayed in Sicily someone might make him as a traitor, and he would surely suffer the consequences. When the war ended with Germany's defeat, Vincentiso migrated to America. At that time, he Anglicized his name to Vic. He also resumed his criminal life after being assimilated into the American mobs of New York City. It did not take long for Gargotta to be noticed by the Czars of Crime for his uncanny abilities as an assassin. He was sent to Kansas City, Missouri, to take care of some problems for the Kansas City mob. Gargotta found Kansas City to his liking and stayed as an enforcer for the Kansas City mob.

In 1939, Gargotta was contacted by a German agent he had known during his capture in Germany. The agent convinced Gargotta that he should accept the money he was being offered from the German government to resume his spying. Otherwise, it could get out that he had betrayed his home country. Gargotta realized he was in a great position to continue his career in crime and make money by spying. He had no qualms about doing both, as money was his objective.

It was Christmas Eve, 1940. Gargotta and a couple of his friends were out celebrating. They had been to numerous bars on the East Twelfth Street area of Kansas City, Missouri. All three of the men were pretty much shit-faced from their consumption of liquor. They had ended up on Twelfth and Vine Streets where they entered the establishment of Jonas Carter, a black businessman and gangster. His saloon was known for good jazz music and was frequented by many of the Negro gangsters of the Kansas City organization.

Jonas had just finished paying his weekly protection money to the police bagmen to ensure that his business could operate twenty-four hours a day without police interference. Gargotta and two friends entered Jonas' bar. One member of the group, Phil Simone, walked to a table where a high dollar card game was in progress and asked to sit in. Gargotta and his other friend seated themselves at the bar, ordered drinks, and listened to the band.

Simone, after losing a few hands and about two hundred dollars, became belligerent and started tossing racial insults at the other card players. Jonas approached Gargotta and informed him that it would be wise for him to get his friend out of the card game and away from the bar before the other patrons and card players took care of it for him. Gargotta got up from his place at the bar, walked over to Simone, and told him it was time to leave.

Simone, now drunk and feeling mean, decided to include Gargotta in his racial slurs. He informed Gargotta that he and all the niggers at the table could go fuck themselves. They were cheating him in the card game, and he wanted their money as well as his. At this point, Simone pulled a small .32 caliber automatic pistol from his waistband. As he did, two of the black men at the card table pulled their guns and emptied their weapons into Simone's chest. He died instantly.

Gargotta, now standing next to the card table, pulled his revolver and stated to the two men who had just killed his friend, "Big mistake!" He then shot both men in the head, killing them instantly. Gargotta, backed up by his other friend, held the patrons in the bar at gunpoint.

Jonas Carter walked up to Gargotta and stated, "You son of a bitch; you will pay for this."

"Do you know who I am and who I work for?" asked Gargotta.

"Yes," replied Carter.

"Then total up your bill and contact me. It will be paid; after that I don't want to hear anything about it from you or your people. Is that understood?"

"Yes," Carter replied.

"You can take care of the cleanup?" mouthed Gargotta.

"Yes," snarled Carter.

Gargotta and his friend then backed out of the tavern, walked to their vehicle, and left the area.

"Holy shit, Vic; I can't believe Simone would pull something like that . . . drunk or sober," his friend said in Italian.

"Simone was short-tempered and stupid, drunk or sober. Sooner or later, he was bound to end up stiff in an alley," replied Vic.

"What are we going to tell the boss? Simone was related to him," asked the friend.

"Fuck the boss; we won't tell him anything. Those niggers won't say anything to anybody. They all know what's what," said Vic in a very harsh tone. "What really worries me," stated Vic, "is what I am going to tell his family when they ask." Vic turned to look at his friend, Anthony Gizzo, and ordered, "You keep your mouth shut."

Chapter Two

Detective Bonacursso, along with his partner, Joseph Ryan, are both members of the Kansas City Missouri homicide unit. They entered the office of Captain James O'Malley and seated themselves in front of his desk. Captain O'Malley was in the process of reading a homicide report handed to him by his Administrative Assistant, Detective Sergeant Walker. As O'Malley read the report, he observed that it had just been completed by the two detectives seated in front of him.

O'Malley looked up and smiled at his two subordinates, then continued reading their report. He read for approximately twenty more minutes. According to the detectives' report, a dozen men, who found themselves at the bottom of the social ladder, remained unaware that they wore a brand of death. A crafty plotter wove their lives into an evil web and waited at the center, like a spider, to feast on his fellow man's flesh.

When the two detectives first saw the cabalistic tattoo, it impressed them only through routine curiosity. It later became a challenge; a lock which no key seemed to fit.

Both detectives Bonacursso and Ryan were in the headquarters building early in the summer of June 1940. Detective Bonacursso had just returned from a long convalescence after being shot with a shotgun in the performance of his duties.

An anonymous caller reported that a bandit, wanted for several crimes—including murder, was hidden in a flophouse at Eighth Street and Troost. This telephone call took them to a squalid district of town, made up of greasy slum joints, nickel grog shops, rescue missions, and hotels reeking of foul odors where canvas cots cost a dime a night, while a cubbyhole cost two times that amount.

Within minutes after receiving the call, the two officers busted into one of these places with guns drawn. A specter, reeking of derail, roused from an iron bed and stared at them in a stupor. Derail was a combination of rotgut alcohol and water, which sold for fifteen cents a pint on the north side of town. Ryan spat in disgust, "This bottle hound couldn't hold up his little finger."

The bum on the bed wheezed, "You'll not refuse an old, sick man the price of coffee and . . ." His voice trailed off and tears glistened in the bloodshot eyes. "It's been three days since I had anything to eat."

The detectives knew this man well as "Crying Hank". After a short conversation, Ryan asked about a strange mark Hank bore on his arm. Ryan took out a small pocket penlight to get a closer look at the tattoo.

"Harry H. Burke," Ryan read aloud. There was a birth date beneath the name and yet another line, "Twenty-eight Nineteen East Ninth, K.C." "Remember?" Ryan prodded.

"Sure," replied Bonacursso, "we made a call on Fifth Street on that D.O.A. It was the same except for the name and date."

The two detectives, feeling something amiss, questioned Hank about the tattoo. Hank told them that a man by the name of Charley Johnson had him put it on his arm.

Bonacursso and Ryan returned to headquarters perplexed. They wondered why tattoos had suddenly become a fad among the rumdums. These alcoholics rarely thought about anything except their next drink. The tattoos stuck in the detectives' minds and could not be dismissed.

A few weeks later, Bonacursso and Ryan were dispatched to another cheap hotel where a dead body had been found. This type of call to a fleabag hotel was not unusual. Dope, rotten liquor, malnutrition, exposure to weather, and sleeping on the sidewalks and in doorways caused a high mortality rate among these people.

The investigation by Detectives Bonacursso and Ryan revealed a man with glassy eyes staring sightlessly at the ceiling. Like many of the others in that district, the detectives knew him. He was known as George "Cyclone" Johnson. Years before, he had been a professional boxer of some repute. He, like many of the derelicts, once enjoyed both success and money. Then he drank everything away and became a bum and a panhandler. Cause of death was apparent, so no autopsy was performed. The alert detectives noticed one unusual thing about the body. On the dead man's right arm was a curious tattoo with his birth date and an address of 2819 East Ninth Street.

Thinking it might be the address of relatives, the detectives went to the two-story residence at 2819 East Ninth Street. They rang the doorbell and waited a few minutes. The gentleman who responded identified himself as Marcus Kaymark. The detectives explained their mission, and Mr. Kaymark informed them that they must have made a mistake. He had never heard of George "Cyclone" Johnson.

Bonacursso and Ryan were in their office reviewing details of the prizefighter's death. After observing the second tattoo on Burk, they stumbled onto another coincidence. They made a telephone call to another officer, a friend who left the department to become an insurance investigator. A few days earlier, they had met their friend emerging from the Carr House at 514 Main Street, another cheap hotel truthfully described as a flophouse. At that meeting, he told the detectives he was looking for someone, but he failed to mention who it was.

"It is George Johnson I am looking for," the insurance investigator informed them over the phone. "So far, no luck. I haven't found any trace of him."

"Come on down," said Ryan. "Maybe we can give you a tip or supply a lead."

Closeted with the detectives, the insurance representative listened to the report about the tattoo on "Crying Hank's" arm and that Charley Johnson told him to have it done. The investigator inquired, "Did you find out where Johnson lives?"

The detectives called on "Crying Hank" again, but the man was unable to give them any helpful information. "Charles Johnson is a swell guy and always willing to pass along the price of a pint. He is a real swell fellow," insisted "Crying Hank", who had earned his nickname for his ability to turn on the tears when he saw an opportunity to mooch a dime.

Charley Johnson, the insurance sleuth told the detectives, was a brother of Cyclone Johnson, the boxer. "My company carried a life insurance policy on the boxer," he explained. "That's why I am trying to locate his brother."

Nearly a week after Bonacursso and Ryan burst in on "Crying Hank", another anonymous telephone call sent them to another flophouse on the trail of the phantom stickup man. They felt the tip was phony, but they could not ignore it. Their raid netted yet another derail-soaked bum who bore the now familiar tattoo. Other false calls followed, but they always found bearers of the tattoos.

The detective team started a search for the artist who had inscribed the tattoos. They soon learned that James Buffet, the operator of a small establishment in a north side hotel, had made the tattoos. When asked if he had been doing work for Charley Johnson, he replied: "Sure, birth date and address." They learned the address was always the same and that Charley always picked up the tab. He gave the detectives more than ten names of those recently tattooed for Charley Johnson.

Detectives Bonacursso and Ryan talked with the insurance investigator about what they learned from the tattoo artist. "Why were you so anxious to talk to Charley Johnson?" they asked.

"It's in regard to a nine hundred dollar policy he had on his brother, the prizefighter," he replied. "You see, a third-party beneficiary collected eight hundred twenty-five dollars. The money was assigned to him as security on a loan he made to Cyclone."

"It makes no sense why anyone would let a north side derelict borrow that much money," replied Ryan.

"There is something wrong as hell," said the insurance man. "My firm can't make a move until we are sure of all the facts."

"Who is the man who loaned Cyclone such a roll?" asked Ryan.

The insurance man looked at some of the papers he held in his hand and informed Ryan and his partner, "It's a dry cleaner named Marcus Kaymark of 2819 East Ninth Street."

The two detectives felt the heat of excitement as they began to gain ground at last, even though they weren't sure how. Both detectives knew they needed to concentrate on the strange cleaning man who bought booze for the north side floaters and later had them tattooed.

However, they lacked enough evidence to bring him into the station for questioning. During their investigation, they learned something of his background. He migrated from Germany and became a naturalized citizen. He was forty-three years of age and came to Kansas City by way of Nashville, Tennessee. After moving to Kansas City, Kaymark worked as an insurance salesman for a short time. He then became a law student.

Armed with this information, they met again with their friend in the insurance business. They learned from him that Kaymark bought several policies on several people. Most of the people were skid row bums. Among the names of those insured was Jerry Flaherty. Mr. Flaherty turned out to be an employee of a cleaning firm in direct competition with Kaymark. He lived with his wife in a small hotel on Independence Avenue. The detective team immediately went there to question Flaherty about Kaymark.

Upon interviewing Flaherty, they learned that he was acquainted with Kaymark and had received a beating at his hands a short time before. Flaherty had been subpoenaed to testify for an insurance company in a case involving Kaymark. Mr. Kaymark also threatened Flaherty and scared him into leaving Kansas City. Flaherty told the detectives that he had been with Kaymark when he gave a pint of derail to Cyclone. He had doped the derail with two white pills. Flaherty had been informed that Cyclone died later. Flaherty also related to the detectives how Kaymark attempted to get extremely friendly with him. He tried to persuade Flaherty to take out an insurance policy on his mother-in-law. When he refused, Kaymark ordered him to leave town; or else.

Ryan and Bonacursso gathered a lot of information, but had no evidence strong enough to substantiate an arrest. The two detectives took their story and information to Detective Sergeant John Walker, their supervisor. He ordered them to stick with the assignment and work on nothing else until they cleared up this wholesale murder mystery. The two detectives returned to the derelicts and began piecing the puzzle together. They found several who had turned Kaymark down on different deals to mark and insure them. They also talked to several men who had been approved by Kaymark to do away with these marked men. The investigation became so involved that it took more than six months to complete. Kaymark was charged with first degree murder and two charges of assault with intent to murder.

O'Malley closed the file and looked at Ryan and Bonacursso. "Nice job on the Kaymark case."

"Thanks," responded both detectives at the same time.

"Do you think you have tied up all the lose ends in this case?" asked O'Malley.

"Yes," replied Ryan.

"Then why are you two looking so glum?"

"Well, boss, we also think the bastard is involved in spying of some sort," snorted Ryan.

"Why do you think that?" inquired O'Malley.

"We found numerous German language documents, linked to the Nazi party, in Kaymark's home. We called in some agents with the Army Intelligence Group, and they snatched up all the papers. Then they refused to tell us anything. When I called our sources in the Army, they told us it was a government problem, not ours, and to keep away from it," stated Ryan.

"So?" replied O'Malley.

"Oh, hell; it just pisses me off to be left out of an investigation that we might have started," stated Ryan, with a sarcastic tone in his voice.

O'Malley smiled. "Don't worry about it, detectives. We will let the Army keep their secrets, as long as they don't interfere with our murder investigation."

Chapter Three

Patrol Officers Mike Conners and James Duffy are both police department veterans of more than ten years. They were assigned to the number two police district as patrol partners for the last two years. They worked the day shift from 7:00 a.m. to 4:00 p.m. Both men enjoyed the assignment, and they also enjoyed each other's company and worked well together. They were assigned to the Country Club District area. Most of the residents ranged from Kansas City's upper class through the extremely wealthy. The worst problems that normally occurred in the area were an occasional speeding vehicle, with a burglary thrown in now and then. At this moment, the officers were parked on a tree-shaded street attempting to keep cool while they pretended to watch the lazy, slow-moving traffic on the street.

Shortly, their radio number 207 was called by the station dispatcher. He advised them to respond to the Cassette Apartments at Fifty-Sixth Street and Broadway. They were to contact the superintendent, who had reported a foul odor. Officer Duffy acknowledged the call and put his unit out-of-service at that location. At the apartment complex they met with Roscoe Vitale, who introduced himself as the apartment complex superintendent. Mr. Vitale stated that he had received numerous complaints of a terrible odor coming from the second floor of the complex. Mr.

Vitale further informed the officers that he was able to check all the apartments on that floor except for apartment number six. He told them that the apartment was rented to a young woman. He thought that she worked at St. Joseph Hospital as a nurse, but he was not sure of that fact. He had noticed that her mail was starting to stack up in her mailbox and that no one had seen her go in or out of her apartment for the past couple of days. Mr. Vitale thought that she might have taken a few days away from the city and forgotten to set her trash out for pickup. He thought that the trash had turned sour and started to smell. He had a master key, but he didn't want to enter the apartment without a witness.

Both officers, along with Mr. Vitale, then walked up the stairway to the second floor. On the second floor, Officer Mike Conners halted the trio and stated to Vitale, "Pal, that ain't no trash or garbage smell. That is the smell of a decaying body."

"Oh, shit!" replied Vitale.

"Roscoe, you stay put while Duffy and I take a look," instructed Officer Conners.

Mr. Vitale handed Conners the master key.

The two uniformed police officers unlocked the door of apartment number six and opened it. The smell permeated the room as the officers entered. In the living room, they observed that a chair was overturned and had what appeared to be blood on the seat area. There also appeared to be blood spatter on the light colored wall, which led to a bedroom. As they entered the bedroom, they observed a woman's bare knees. She was lying on the floor beyond the bed. Only her bare knees showed above the level of the mattress. The mattress appeared to be new, and was still wrapped in light colored paper.

The two cops stared. The unmoving knees were all they could see. The smell was definitely that of a dead, decomposing body. Both officers now entered the bedroom for a closer look. The mattress had slid part way off the bed and rested on top of the victim's face. The victim had a stocking stuffed into her mouth. Her arms were above her head, under the bed, and her bra and sweater were tangled around her elbows. The woman's underarms were smooth-shaven, and she had small, beautiful breasts. She was lying, knees spread, as if eager to receive a man. Around her neck was a red necktie, knotted tightly. The color was gone from the rest of her flesh. The part of her face that Conners and Duffy could see was engorged red.

Her hair was coal black. The woman's skin was flawless, except for some pink and purplish bruises on her thighs. She had very pale, rather small areolas. In life, this woman probably had an exciting figure, though no one would ever know again how her body looked standing. The orifice between her legs gaped, as if her lover had just withdrawn. She looked to be in her mid- to late twenties.

Neither Officer Conners nor his partner had ever seen a death involving what appeared to be a rape. The sight and the smell caused Conners to vomit his breakfast. This, in turn, caused Duffy to do the same. Once Conners composed himself, he informed Mr. Vitale what they had discovered and stated that it was now a crime scene. He then called his supervisor and notified the Homicide Unit.

Two detectives responded first, followed by many more. The District Commander and his staff also responded. As each man entered the front door, they could look straight down the corridor, into the bedroom, and at the victim. As the detectives worked the crime scene, they moved back and forth, occasionally blocking the view. The first glimpse of her, from a distance, was of shins, inner thighs, and pubic hair. This seemed incomprehensible. Why was she lying there naked when there were so many men in her room, all fully clothed?

Each new detective entering the bedroom stared down wordlessly. At arm's length from her right hip, against the wall, lay a used sanitary napkin. The victim could not move to hide it, and no one else did.

Officers Conner and Duffy were standing in the doorway writing their report, listing the names of all those who entered and left the apartment. They remained at this task until relieved by the on-scene detective supervisor, who in this case was Detective Sergeant John Walker.

Detective Sergeant John Walker, a red-headed Irishman of fifty-two, was already one of the police department's legions in crime investigation. He had been in the homicide unit most of his police career. He stood six foot two inches and weighed in at two hundred pounds of pure muscle. He was educated in the Kansas City public school system and attended and graduated from Kansas City Business College. He joined the police force at the age of twenty-six and aspired to the rank of detective. He then transferred to the homicide unit where he was partnered up with the crime and corruption fighter, Lieutenant James O'Malley.

O'Malley had recently been promoted to Captain of the Homicide Division. These two men worked extremely well together. Within a week of his promotion, O'Malley had Walker re-assigned to the Homicide Unit as a Detective Sergeant directly under him. Walker was the second in charge of all homicide investigations.

He looked down at the red tie knotted around her throat. Walker slid the mattress back on the bed. The woman's face was now uncovered. Her eyes were closed. Her mouth was open and still stuffed with a stocking. A closer examination showed blood on her teeth. Her checks were blotchy and red; her face was contorted with fear, pain, and anger. She had been a beautiful woman, evident even in her death struggle. She had fought her assailant. The bruises on her legs and her bloody mouth attested to that.

Walker ordered his detectives to go through her closets, drawers, jewelry, and underwear. They collected any and all things deemed suspicious in the crime scene. The invasion of her privacy was total, but it would get worse.

The reporters were beginning to arrive at the scene and were demanding information. They wanted access to the crime scene, but were denied by Sergeant Walker. Hours passed while the detectives worked. All the while, the woman still lay in her death position. Detectives stepped back and forth over her body. As far as they were concerned, the young woman was just another piece of furniture in the room.

Seven hours into the crime scene investigation, Walker released the body to the coroner's ambulance, and she was transported to the morgue for examination. The crime laboratory unit had responded to the scene and was assisting the homicide unit with photographs and evidence collecting. They would be at the scene for several more hours.

At last the stretcher came into the room, and the attendants lifted the body onto it. She was stiff. The attendants put their hands on her knees and leaned on her, straightening out her long, slim legs. The red tie remained knotted around her throat. While on the stretcher, a sheet was wrapped around her. She was then removed to the morgue for a more thorough examination by the coroner.

Once at the morgue, the stretcher belts were undone, and the sheets were removed and checked for evidence by a waiting detective. Her clothing was removed and examined.

She was laid on a slab under bright lights and photographed by the detectives. The medical examiner entered the autopsy room and started his examination, dictating to a stenographer as he did. The detectives stood in attendance at the woman's autopsy. No dark humor escaped any of their lips as they witnessed the event. The detectives all realized the seriousness of the autopsy. The witnessing detectives were all in their fifties and had families . . . some had daughters of their own who were the same age as the victim. They all realized that, but for the grace of God, any of them might have a daughter on that slab.

"This is the body of a well-nourished, well-developed twenty-five year old white female," stated the attending pathologist. He went on to describe the color of her nipples and the color of her pubic hair and other incidentals—then got down to business. "Death was apparently due to strangulation caused by a tightly knotted red tie." The pathologist handed the red tie to the detective who was collecting evidence and then continued his examination. He examined the vagina and noted the number, extent, and location of various small tears in the membranes along with the quantity of semen deposited there. He then opened her up with his scalpel and noted the quality and quantity of urine in her bladder and the contents of her intestines. He weighed and sliced her liver, and then sent it to the laboratory for further examination. The pathologist noted the condition of her ovaries, and then removed several vials of blood to go to the laboratory along with the other body parts.

He then examined her head by cutting away the rear skull cap. He pulled the skin over her head and down over her face. He removed the skull, which made a snapping sound. He removed her brain and weighed and dissected it. The face was then pulled down and away from the bone and nasal area. Fractures were noted. The facial skin and skull skin was pulled back over her head, making her appear worse than when brought to the morgue. The doctor, having finished, left her side and walked over to autopsy another body which had been involved in a fatal traffic accident.

By now, the detectives working the case knew she was a nurse and that she had just signed a lease on the apartment where she was found. She was having new furniture delivered, and she had been working on the apartment for at least the last ten days. She had gone to nursing school after high school and was employed by St. Joseph Hospital. She normally did not date, although she was a very beautiful and popular young woman.

Chapter Four

Early in the morning, Gargotta had reported to his boss, Zino Torrio. Gargotta thought that Zino had found out somehow that he and Anthony Gizzo had been involved in the death of Simone and the disruption of a mob-controlled bar. Torrio owned a bakery in the middle of Little Italy, and this is where he held court on all the mob's business. Prior to arriving at Torrio's bakery, Gargotta made sure he had the .38 caliber in his waistband. He didn't think Torrio would harm him while he was in the bakery, especially at the busiest time of the day. However, you never knew for sure with a crazy son-of-a-bitch like Torrio.

The bakery was a two-story block long building. The baking of the products that were offered throughout the city was done in the rear of the building with a large retail area that sold all types of Italian foods. Upstairs over the retail office was Zino Torrio's office. This is where he held court and made all the decisions concerning the criminal activities of the Kansas City mob. As Gargotta climbed the back stairs to Torrio's office, he noticed two burly bodyguards standing at the doorway of Torrio's office. As the two guards noticed Gargotta, they became stiff and alert. One of the thugs approached Gargotta and patted him down, finding his gun. He pulled it from his waistband and stated, "Vic, you know the rules. No weapons up here."

At this time Gargotta replied, "Just an old habit."

Gargotta was told that when he left, his gun would be returned to him. The second thug then knocked on Torrio's door and announced that Gargotta was waiting.

Gargotta then entered Torrio's office. He realized that the office was actually much larger than it looked. Next to the door sat Torrio's secretary, who was actually nothing more than another thug used as a bodyguard. He had the distinction of being a close personal friend of Torrio by the name of Joe Caruso. Caruso always watched all the proceedings going on while Zino dealt with people. The thug again searched Gargotta and motioned for him to walk over to the second door, knock, and enter. Caruso stated, "Open the door and go on in."

This area of the office had a simple large desk in the middle of the room. There were no rugs, only hardwood floors—not a very impressive place for a businessman to work. However, it sufficed for the activities of the mob. Zino was sitting at this desk, engrossed in writing on some type of document. Torrio looked up at Gargotta with a menacing stare on his face. Gargotta, for the first time, felt the heat of fear. He knew Torrio ruled his world and would take no shit from a two-bit hood for any reason.

"What have you been up to, my friend?" questioned Torrio with his Italian accent.

"Just the usual, don Torrio." Realizing that Torrio did not know about the killing of Simone by the tone of his voice and his question, Gargotta decided not to bring it up.

"I've got a job for you, Vic."

"I'm always at your disposal, don Torrio," replied Gargotta.

"I want you to handle a small problem I have with a pimp who manages a whore house on Seventh Street. His name is Joseph Candanza. This fucker has shortchanged us for the last year. I want you to retire him permanently."

"Don Torrio, what time frame do you want this done in?"

"I give you five days."

"Done," replied Gargotta.

"Don't let me down, or you'll never let me down again."

Torrio then continued scribbling on his document. Gargotta knew he had been dismissed. Therefore, he turned and walked out the door into the hallway, retrieving his weapon from the bodyguard.

That evening, Gargotta checked out the business area of the retiring Mr. Joe Candanza. He was a young pimp who had made some good money working for Torrio. He had, however, decided to double-cross him by holding out on the profits. Gargotta figured Candanza cut his own throat with the mob, and now he was going to cut it for him. Of all racketeering activities, prostitution carried the greatest stigma to a gangster's reputation. Yet it formed a vital part of his initiation into the rackets. Prostitution was not merely a sideline of the rackets, it was the foundation. For racketeers, especially the higher-ups, it carried an aura of disgrace. Those who derived their fortune from brothels habitually deviated attention from the ugly fact by pointing to the hypocrisies of those who sought to suppress vice. In the end, they could never mount an adequate defense of what they did. They could only insist that people always wanted illicit sexual activity; it was human nature; and someone was going to make money from it. They might as well be the ones to cash in.

During surveillance, Gargotta observed the building was an old brick, two-story, flat-roofed building. It was weather-beaten and unpainted, as were all the other buildings in that area of Seventeenth Street. It was rumored that it was one of the most profitable in Torrio's group of brothels.

Victor Gargotta walked through the front door of the building, where he confronted several women about twenty years old who wore flimsy undergarments called teddies. Some wore fishnet hose, and others wore knee-high stockings. On their feet were high-heeled pumps of varying colors to enhance them sexually. As he walked through the door, a hostess greeted him and informed him that for $2.00 he could enjoy any one of the girls, and for $5.00 he could have two girls at the same time. The hostess then took Gargotta's hand and led him to a small cubicle. It contained a very small bed with linen that appeared to be clean-to-dirty, depending on how you looked at it. There was a table with a cheap bowl and pitcher of water, a towel, a bar of soap, and a small 25-watt electric bulb hanging from the ceiling. The hostess asked Gargotta, "You want a first-class fuck and blow job for $3.00, or just a $2.00 trick?" The hostess then informed Gargotta she would throw in a rubber to counteract any venereal disease for an additional 25 cents.

Gargotta knew from prior experience that if he didn't become a customer, he would not get any further into the building. He then told the hostess that all he wanted was a nice, easy blow job—which she gave him. After paying her $3.00, he handed her another $2.00 as an extra gratuity. He then told her he needed a drink and was directed to the upstairs bar.

A saloon occupied the first floor, where locally produced whiskey sold for 25 cents and imported whiskey sold for 75 cents. The imported variety came from the brothel next door, probably out of the same bathtub as the local variety.

On the second floor were a horse-betting parlor and a gambling den consisting of poker, roulette, faro, and blackjack. A closed-off office area was adjacent to a set of billiard tables where Joe Candanza managed the entire operation.

Gargotta had a clear, close view of the door to Candanza's office from his vantage at the bar. He observed the comings and goings of numerous politicians, cops looking for a favor or a payoff, and whores who wanted to work in his brothel with the protection it offered from the normal hazards of the vice world. Although Gargotta had never met or seen Candanza, he had memorized a description and recognized him the second he observed the man walk out of his office. Candanza was dressed impeccably in a blue serge suit, black shoes which were highly shined, white shirt, and striped tie. His hair was jet black and combed straight back. On his right wrist he wore an expensive watch, and the ring fingers on both hands sported diamond rings. He also wore a shoulder holster under his coat. Gargotta figured that the wiseguy most likely was armed with some type of .380 caliber weapon. It seemed to be the weapon preferred by most pimps. Candanza walked with an irritating swagger, typical of a smart-ass gangster who thought his shit didn't stink.

Gargotta finished his drink and left the bar area to walk out to the street. He observed the building from every angle, and came to the conclusion that Candanza could not be taken at the brothel without problems. He would have to find another way to take him. For now, he walked to his automobile, entered the vehicle, and observed the activity generated at an active whore house. A few hours later, Gargotta observed Candanza exit his business and walk alone toward a new Ford two-door coupe parked at the curb near the front door of the brothel. Gargotta also realized that Candanza's vehicle was being guarded by a tough looking hood, who opened the driver's door for him. Candanza then drove away by himself. No one followed him—except for Gargotta.

Gargotta followed his target to the east side of town, where he watched as Candanza stopped at a large two-story residence which obviously belonged to a wealthy citizen. Candanza got out and entered the house with that irritating swagger which Gargotta had really grown to dislike in the past couple of hours. Candanza soon reappeared, walked to his vehicle, and entered. Gargotta had parked his car about twenty yards to the rear, with his motor idling. He slowly put the car in gear and pulled up next to Candanza. He then pulled in front—pinning Candanza at the curb. Gargotta jumped out of his car, and Candanza did the same. Candanza walked toward Gargotta, yelling, "What the fuck do you think you are . . ."

"Hold on, Joe; I'm a detective from downtown. I'm supposed to give you a message—if you don't shoot me," stated Gargotta.

"What message; from who?" replied Candanza. He now relaxed his grip and left his weapon in the holster.

Gargotta, with unbelievable reflexes, produced a six-inch stiletto and advanced on Candanza. He jabbed the blade into Candanza's right eye—then with lightning speed, into the upper chest of the victim. This left the injured man with the wind completely knocked from his body. Before Candanza even felt the pain, Gargotta was behind the victim and cut his throat from ear-to-ear. Blood spurted onto Gargotta, covering his suit and shirt. As Candanza fell to his knees, Gargotta stabbed him two more times in the chest. As Candanza's blood spilled onto the sidewalk, Gargotta knelt in front of the dying man and looked into his face. He stated, "The boss said you are retired, you cheap fucking pimp." Gargotta then reached into Candanza's breast pocket and removed a fat envelope full of one hundred dollar bills. He placed the cash in his own breast pocket, walked to his automobile, and drove away.

Chapter Five

Police Officer William Toler had recently been assigned to the east patrol division. The station house was next to the east fire station on Fifteenth Street and Belmont, located in the industrial area of the city. He had transferred from a downtown foot beat, where he had been assigned since his academy graduation two years earlier. Upon arriving at his new assignment, Toler was partnered up on patrol (in a two-man police car) with a man whom no other veteran officer would work with. He was a drunk and a slacker, and he should have been fired long before. He was appointed by the city controlled police department and had paid his dues by amassing a large vote for the political party in power. Therefore, he was tolerated by his supervisors. Hell, even the supervisors were drunks or were known to do a little stealing now and then. Although the police department was now under State control, the residue of city control remained.

Toler and his new partner, Joseph Smith, started their tour of duty at 1600 hours and normally ended at midnight. They were working this month on what was known as the third watch. They had been issued a new 1940 Ford four-door—black with a white hood and trunk. The word POLICE was painted on the door in bold letters. The vehicle was equipped with a red light and siren to warn traffic out of the way. They had one of the newest radios in the police department, which was connected to the station house. One of the unwritten laws of the police department was that the senior officer got to pick whether he drove or rode. If the senior officer elected to ride and allowed the younger officer to drive, then the senior officer was to take all the reports and handle the radio calls for the unit. However, senior police officer Smith was usually too intoxicated and abusive to the public to drive or take the written reports. Toler handled both. Smith usually stayed in the car and took a little nip of liquor.

Their tour of duty started with their response to a residential burglary. Toler wrote the report while Smith remained in the vehicle. They were then sent on an armed robbery. Upon arrival, Toler again took the report and then turned the crime scene over to the district detectives for investigation. Both officers agreed that it was time to take a coffee break. They proceeded to a small diner on Fifteenth Street and Spruce. Toler parked the car and went to grab two cups of coffee. While sitting in the patrol car, they received a call from the station house that a disturbance of some sort had occurred two blocks east of their location. They were ordered to check it out.

Gargotta had just started to pull away from the curb when he noticed a couple of men running from the house where his victim had just exited. They appeared to be armed, and one of them started shooting in his direction. He accelerated down the road at a high rate of speed. During his escape, Gargotta lost control of his vehicle and struck a parked car. In the process, he tore a front fender from his automobile. As luck would have it, his hit-and-run was witnessed by both Officer Toler and his partner as they were responding to the reported disturbance. Toler decided that the disturbance call could wait and gave chase to the hit-and-run vehicle.

Gargotta chose to travel side streets at high rates of speed, but he realized he could not outrun the cops. He thought if he didn't do something quickly, he would have a lot more of them on him. He chose to stop his car and deal with his pursuers. He placed his revolver in his lap, out of sight, and waited for the officers to catch up with him. Officers Toler and Smith pulled in behind Gargotta, and both officers exited the police car. Smith remained behind, locating himself at the rear of Gargotta's car. Toler approached the driver's side with his weapon drawn. He then ordered Gargotta out of the vehicle.

Gargotta pretended to be intoxicated and acted confused. He began to slur his words for effect. Thinking that he had just captured a drunk hit-and-run suspect, Toler lowered his gun and relaxed. He yelled to Smith that it was just a damn drunk. Toler then opened the driver's side door and told the drunk to get out of the vehicle.

Like a cat, the gangster exited the vehicle and shot Officer Toler in the middle of his forehead. The shot blew the back of his head into the street—killing him instantly. He then shot Smith point-blank in the chest several times. Smith fell to the street dead. Gargotta then jumped back into his vehicle and drove away from the scene. The bodies of both officers were left lying on the street in front of their police car.

Chapter Six

H is slight physique, at five foot eight inches, one hundred fifty pounds, with lean strong muscles, indicates at once to an observer that this man keeps himself in outstanding physical shape. He is fifty-eight years old, but could pass for a much younger man. He looked to be no more than in his late thirties. This man had cold blue eyes that, if staring at you, would cause shivers to run up and down your spine. He had light brown hair with just a sprinkle of gray at the temple. This made it difficult to guess an age with any certainty. This person had been known as Peter Morgan for the past fifteen years.

Peter Morgan had been educated at Harvard University, where he studied law and political science. Morgan then went on to law studies and graduated in the top of his law class. He then went on to receive his PhD in jurisprudence and political science while also teaching classes at the University. Mr. Morgan became very active in many of the politics in Boston, Massachusetts, and at the University. Peter enjoyed the academic life and the freedom that went with it. It allowed him to be admired and respected by members of the political party of the President of the United States, Mr. Franklin D. Roosevelt.

Today he was stepping off of the train at Kansas City, Missouri, into the Union Station. He was dressed in a dark navy blue three-piece custom made suit with highly polished black shoes. He was quite a distinguished looking person. Morgan wore a pair of round framed eyeglasses, which distracted from his eyes. This gave him the look of a busy and harmless attorney or that of a successful banker or businessman. He also carried a brown leather briefcase and sported a gray fedora on his head. This appearance set him off as a dapper looking educator. This was the identity that most of his associates saw.

However, Mr. Morgan's name was nothing more than an alias to hide his real identity. Peter Morgan was born in Berlin, Germany, to a prominent family that produced numerous lawyers, businessmen, doctors, and military people. His family was extremely wealthy and well-connected with the German Government. Morgan's true name was Auto Van Kessler. He was educated at the Heidelberg University where, at the age of nineteen, he obtained his PhD in politics and language. He was an outstanding student with an I.Q. of 190 and always at the top of his classes. Kessler, while at Heidelberg University, met and became close friends with Paul Joseph Gobbels. He was introduced to the Nazi movement through his friend Gobbels.

Kessler associated with many of the leaders of the Nazi party and, in 1925, was befriended by Heinrick Himmler. At that time he was recruited to the German Intelligence and became an SS Officer. He was then sent to the United States to study and gather as much information about the U.S. and its people as possible. He was given the new identity of Peter Morgan. He spoke perfect English and was thought to have been born in Boston, Massachusetts. This worked well for his hidden agenda. His passport was American, although this phony passport did not show that he had ever been in Germany. Morgan had a second passport with his real name that he used when traveling to his homeland, where he reported over the years to his boss Himmler.

While at Harvard University, Morgan was promoted by Himmler to the rank of SS Obergruppenflses. Kessler had earned, during his time in the German Army, decorations which included the Blood Order, Golden Party Badge, Combined Pilots-Observation

Badge, SS Long Service Award, Anschluss Commemorative Medal, Sudetenland Medical Award, Memel Medal, Totenkipf Ring, and SS Honor Sword. He had recently been awarded the Award of the Iron Cross for his intelligence work for Germany. In his briefcase Morgan carried orders concerning his duties in Kansas City.

Morgan's orders were simple, but encompassed a wide area of activity to be performed under his direction. He was to engage in intensive efforts to obtain military, economic, and political information concerning the United States and establish extensive espionage networks. He was to cause large scale sabotage relating to war production, shipping, and obtain technical advancements.

Morgan, as an SS Intelligence Officer, carried in his head the secret intelligence requirements of the German High Command under the Third Reich. It was served by a separate branch other than its Armed Forces. The branch was the AMT Auslands and Abwehr. This group was independent of the three service commands: Army, Navy, and Air Services. Each of these three maintained their own intelligence staff for the evaluation and dissemination of information obtained from both open and secret sources. None of these branches conducted any secret intelligence activities themselves. They maintained liaison with the Abwehr to which their special needs for information were made known.

The Abwehr endeavored to meet their requests. At the same time they were engaged in the task of collecting, on a worldwide scale, all manner of information which could be of interest to the High Command or the individual services subordinate thereto.

The Abwehr was divided into three basic groups called Abteilung. One of the groups was charged with offensive intelligence, including espionage. Another group was in charge of sabotage and subversion, and a third with counterintelligence and security. Group one of the Abteilung was broken down into sections cognizant respectively over military, naval, air, and economic intelligence, plus certain technical sections. These sections were further broken down into geographical subsections, dealing with particular countries or areas. In addition to the headquarter's organizations in Berlin, the Abwehr maintained field offices in Germany and abroad, staffed by Abwehr Officers. In

Germany and occupied countries, these field offices were referred to as Abwehrstellen, with branches there called Nebenstellen. In neutral countries the Abwehr office was called a Kriegsorganisation and usually acted under cover of the diplomatic mission. The field stations reproduced the functional division at headquarters. Both headquarters and the field stations recruited, trained, and dispatched espionage agents for missions abroad. While in theory there was a rough geographical division of responsibility between the various Abwehrstellen, in practice there was a great deal of overlapping.

Side by side with the Abwehr there existed another intelligence agency called the Sicherheitsdienst. It was originally the security and intelligence service of the Nazi Party. It had the dominant role of an intelligence organ of the Reich and had control over the Abwehr itself. In 1939, the Sicherheitsdienst was brought together with various police agencies of Germany, including the Gestapo, to form the Reichssicherheitshauptanf, the central security service of the Reich. It was now all controlled by the Nazi Party SS.

Morgan had all this information in his head and knew that, if captured, he would have to terminate his own existence. While he was in Boston, he had been contacted by an Agent of the Abwehr, who passed on to him top secret assignments. He carried them with him in his briefcase on this day. The assignment in his briefcase listed targets to work and an order that included an assassination of an agent in Kansas City. This agent was in the custody of the Kansas City Missouri Police Department, and he was charged with numerous homicides. He was thought to have contacted the American Army Intelligence people to make a deal for information concerning the German intelligence organization.

Chapter Seven

Morgan walked to the baggage area, where he contacted a black porter dressed in a bright red and gold uniform. Morgan gave the porter his baggage claim ticket, instructing the man to bring his bags to the east cab area. He also instructed the porter to have his bags at the cab stand in about twenty minutes. Morgan handed the porter five dollars. The porter smiled and stated, "Yes, sir; twenty minutes."

Morgan walked up the massive stairs of white and gray marble to the train lobby. While standing in the lobby, he checked to make sure that no one was following him. He watched for a few moments and found no one suspicious or out of place. Morgan then walked over to an information counter and obtained a Union Station history pamphlet. The information in the pamphlet indicated that he was at Thirty West Pershing Road, and the architect was Jarvis Hunt, a proponent of the City Beautiful Program. The design of the train station is a main hall for ticketing and a perpendicular hall extending over the tracks for waiting passengers. According to the pamphlet, the station opened for business on October 30, 1914. It was the second largest train station in the United States. The building encompassed eight hundred fifty thousand square feet. The ceiling in the Grand Hall was ninety-five feet high with three massive chandeliers weighing thirty-five hundred pounds each. The clock mounted in the Grand Hall had a six foot diameter face.

Due to the Union Station's central location, Kansas City was the hub for both passenger and freight rail traffic. Union Station made headlines on June 17, 1933, as four unarmed Federal Bureau of Investigation Agents were gunned down by gang members attempting to free a captured fugitive named Frank Nash. Nash was also killed in the gun battle. This incident resulted in the arming of all Federal Bureau of Investigation Agents.

The traffic through this station averaged 678,363 annually and had not yet reached its peak in traffic.

Morgan/Kessler thought to himself that he would never be caught without his firearm. He always carried his weapon in a left-handed shoulder holster. His weapon of choice was a 9mm Walther P38 parabellum. Morgan was very effective with his weapon.

Morgan walked around the Grand Hall for approximately fifteen minutes, looking surreptitiously around to see if he was being followed or watched. He observed no one. He then walked toward the east taxi area. The porter was waiting with his luggage. The cabbie took the bags from the porter, and Morgan handed the porter another five dollars for the extra trouble. Morgan then entered the cab.

The cabdriver, a white male in his forties, asked "Where to?"

Morgan replied, "Aladdin Hotel, you know it?"

"Yes, sir," replied the driver. "You know it's the tallest building in Kansas City—built around 1925. It is sixteen stories tall. Isn't that something? The Continental Hotel is also nice; it's just a few blocks north of the Aladdin." The driver was hoping to get some extra money for the ride and his suggestion.

"No, my friend. I have already made a reservation at the Aladdin. I am meeting some business associates there."

Upon arrival at the hotel, the driver pulled in front and a porter removed Morgan's baggage and opened the taxi door for him. They both entered the hotel after Morgan paid the cabdriver the fare of three dollars and tipped him two dollars more. At the hotel counter, he signed the register as required by law. A key was given to his porter, and Morgan was led to an elevator and taken to the twelfth floor and his apartment number 1202. The porter opened the door with the key and allowed Morgan to enter the room ahead of him. The porter placed the suitcases on the bed and then showed Morgan the apartment. Upon receiving his tip, the porter thanked him and told him that if he needed anything he should call the front desk. The porter then left the room and Morgan was alone with his thoughts.

Chapter Eight

$\mathcal{D}$etective Sergeant Johnson was at his desk in the Homicide Unit of the Headquarters Building reviewing reports. He was also listening to the police reporter and some of his detectives who were sitting at the squad table waiting for the show up of arrested suspects who had been picked up the previous night. Normally on week day mornings at eight o'clock, the detectives would sit in the darkened front row of the police "show up" room and watch the parade of suspects onto a lighted stage. The suspects were questioned briefly as the detectives, unseen by the suspects, studied their faces and learned their records. The "show up" was open only to members of the police department or representatives of other law enforcement agencies. Usually, only the city detectives entered the room.

The detectives and the reporter were telling each other tall tale stories that they always claimed were true. In fact, they were usually, but not always, made up. These stories in the police jargon were known as "war stories". The police reporter, William Stipa, related a story he had heard about a young patrolman whom he refused to identify. This meant that it was about someone in the office or someone known to all present. Stipa wanted to embarrass that person without revealing his or her identity. Stipa stated, "For months a youthful, slender motorcycle patrolman wore a teeny weenie mustachio, which was his pride and joy. There were those among his public who made rude, merry, or sarcastic quips, such as 'growing vegetation' or 'a baseball team—nine whiskers on each side'. When such remarks reached the sensitive ears of this patrolman, his face would color and frequent fist fights ensued. One time this officer of the law finished second in defending his sprouting mustachio. He was ganged in a night club and slugged unconscious. The news was enough for the Police Chief to order the patrolman to shave off the mustache or he would fire the young officer. The officer saluted the chief, then hustled to a photographer. 'Mug me,' cried the patrolman while tenderly touching his upper lip. 'That is, if this will show up.'

Maybe to forget and maybe not, the young officer took up revolver practice in a big way. He worked countless hours at the police target range. He finally won a medal, inscribed 'expert marksman' for being the best shot of the traffic division.

A month later, the patrolman, coatless and off-duty, stood in the parlor of his home. His right arm was extended, fingers clutching a revolver, squinting along the barrel. All of a sudden he heard his sister's voice behind him asking what he was doing. 'I am dry-shooting,' he replied.

'What do you mean dry-shooting?' asked the sister.

'Dry-shooting is what we sharpshooters call keeping in practice in our spare moments with unloaded guns, like mine.' He nodded towards a nearby table on which lay six lead-nosed cartridges. 'Then,' he resumed, 'we aim at some object and pull the trigger—again and again. That is dry-shooting. It keeps eye and finger muscles in good condition.'

'You'd better stop that dry-shooting business and head for work; you are late now,' she told him.

The officer sighed as he placed his weapon on the table and entered a bedroom. He put on the uniform blouse and cap. His sister was in the kitchen when her brother returned to the parlor and picked up his revolver. He patted it affectionately, then muttered, 'I'll squeeze it just once more.' He did and 'Boom!' The officer's sister, trying to speed her brother's departure to work, had reloaded the revolver when he went after his coat and cap. As for the bullet fired by the startled officer . . . where did it go? Well, hadn't he been aiming at a small, round frame hanging on a wall ten feet away? Wasn't he the crack shot of the motorcycle and traffic squads?

He glanced ruefully at the jagged hole in the plaster. He lifted the smashed picture frame from the floor. The officer and expert shot had scored a bull's eye; he had shot off the photographed mustachio of himself in a police uniform!"

The detectives all broke into hardy belly laughs over this story. Detective Ryan, who has been with the department for the last fifteen years, stated, "I would like to know the name of that stupid son-of-a-bitch and how long after that incident did it take for him to get fired?"

The reporter looked into the eyes of the detective with a straight face and stated loud enough for the whole squad room to hear, including Detective Supervisor Johnson, "Your captain."

"No shit," replied Detective Ryan.

"No shit," replied the reporter.

Detective Mike James, a large heavyset officer known for street fighting and speedy fists, followed with his own story. "Once, a shabbily dressed stranger, his eyes a pale and smoky gray, timidly entered a lawyer's office and seated himself on the edge of his chair. 'I'm an old, old man,' the visitor began shyly, his hat in hand. 'I won't be here long. Please be so kind as to draw up my will.' The lawyer asked for a detailed statement of the bequest. 'Well, I'm a widower with seven fine children,' the visitor continued. 'I would like to leave $50,000.00 to my eldest son John.' The attorney jotted down the name and amount. 'I would like to leave $50,000.00 each to Bob, Dick, and Chauncey.' The attorney's pen moved again. 'To my daughters: Mary, Helen, and Bernice, I would like to leave $50,000.00 each.' The man spoke with a masterful air of finality. Astonished, the lawyer lowered his glasses.

'Beg pardon,' the lawyer said at last, 'but you certainly fooled me; you certainly did. From your appearance, I was sure you had no money. Appearances are deceptive. Quite an estate you have,

$350,000.00! Well, well; I'll ring for my stenographer and we will draw up your will.'

'Just a moment,' interrupted the stranger, rising from the chair. 'I said I would like to leave my children $50,000.00 each, and indeed I would like to. Please, could you give me a dime?'"

Laughter again broke out in the squad room.

The reporter, not to be outdone by the detectives, had this story to tell. "A man wearily dragged himself to the city hospital and went to bed. He stayed there two weeks. Physicians examined him and went away shaking their heads. Atwood, that was his name, complained of many ills. It was a puzzling case. The doctors looked at his tongue. They examined the color of his eyes. They took his temperature. Atwood took it easy. It certainly was a puzzling case. One doctor decided that Atwood might be afflicted with hookworm. They turned the patient over to the Helping Hand Institute. The Helping Hand Institute turned Atwood over to the kitchen boss. Atwood turned over a few dishes. Then he went back to the hospital. 'I'm a sick man,' he cried. 'Put me to bed.' Again physicians examined him with stethoscopes and thermometers. It certainly was a puzzling case. Then the physicians decided that the best remedy had been neglected. Atwood was sent to the municipal court via the policeman stationed at the hospital. They had concluded that Atwood was a loiterer and loafer and had wasted the time of the physicians on duty at the hospital.

The judge asked Atwood a leading question, one which had been overlooked by all the specialists in making their diagnosis. 'Do you like to work?'

'No,' Atwood responded.

'Try one hundred days on the rock pile,' ordered the judge."

Laughter could be heard throughout the squad room and hallway to the show up room as the detectives headed for the day's lineups.

Chapter Nine

William (Bill) Cosgrove was just leaving his home and walking to his place of employment at the Iron Works of Kansas City. The day was starting out to be cloudy and cool, with the scent of moisture in the air. He lived just over two miles from where he worked, and for the last several years he had walked the distance.

Bill heard in the distance the sound of a police siren coming toward him as he turned off of his home street onto St. John Avenue. He was walking east toward Belmont Street, and the siren was coming toward him from the west. As Cosgrove neared Belmont Street, he looked in the direction of the siren's sound and observed a vehicle being chased by a marked police car. Both automobiles passed him traveling at a high rate of speed. The cars turned south on Belmont Street with their tires screaming into the turn. The vehicle being chased by the police was a gray Ford, maybe a 1936 Model four-door with damage to the front of the car. Cosgrove also thought that the front bumper and maybe the left fender were missing. He had further noticed that the Ford was driven by a white man.

The second automobile was a black and white police car, running with its red light and siren. Two policemen appeared to be in the car. They disappeared around the corner, where the siren stopped.

Shortly Bill Cosgrove thought he heard the sounds of gun fire. Then nothing else. So Cosgrove thought to himself that the officers had decided to shoot at the fleeing vehicle. But he heard nothing else. It was Sunday and there was no other traffic in the area. He decided that it probably wasn't the police shooting at the fleeing car and driver but the sound of trains passing in the area. Cosgrove pulled his pocket watch out of his bib overalls and saw that it was 11:00 a.m. He had half an hour to get to work.

Approximately ten minutes later, as Bill Cosgrove approached Manchester Street that led to the Kansas City Iron Works, he observed the black and white police car stopped with its red light on. It was standing in the middle of the street. Bill walked on the shoulder of the road as there were no sidewalks at this location. He also observed two uniformed policemen laying in pools of thick, dark red blood. Bill Cosgrove, instead of checking to see whether he could help the officers, ran past them for two more blocks. He located a pay phone booth and called the police station.

The police officer who took the phone call from Bill told him to return to the police car and wait for other officers who would be en route.

Three police units, upon hearing the radio call "Officers down, Assist the Officer" and the approximate location, responded without delay using both their red lights and sirens. In the world of law enforcement the most dreaded call is the "Assist the officer". It means that an officer is in deep trouble of a dangerous nature and his life depends upon the help of other officers. These types of calls could bring as many as twenty police units to the location where help was requested at quick time speed.

The first police unit arrival on the scene was Policeman Henry Wilcox, a ten-year veteran on the force, and his partner Robert Shaw, another seasoned officer. They witnessed that the crime scene looked unreal with the two uniformed policemen laying in a pool of blood in the street in front of their police unit. Officer Wilcox checked the bodies of the officers for signs of life and realized that he knew both men. He checked Officer Smith first and then Officer Toler. Both were dead—apparently the victims of gunshots. The two responding officers would need the District Captain and Homicide Detectives to respond to their location ASAP!

All the activity had started to draw numerous spectators to the crime scene. The officers at the scene had become spectators themselves and they stood around in a daze thinking except for the grace of God this could be them.

Captain James O'Malley was at his desk talking to a lawyer about a case that was getting ready for trial when his telephone rang. The caller was Sergeant Wayne Anderson of the East Police District. He sounded like he was out of breath with excitement. "Captain, my officers were dispatched to the East Iron Works on Belmont Street just under the railroad bridge on an 'Assist the officer' call. When they arrived they found that two of our uniformed officers had been shot to death. We are requesting your unit to handle the incident."

"Right," said O'Malley. "They will be en route to the scene. Be sure to have the senior officer at the scene protect the area. It will take us about twenty to thirty minutes."

O'Malley hung up the phone, stood up from his chair, and headed to the show-up room. He pulled Detective Sergeant John Walker out of the room, informed him of the incident, and instructed him to get Detectives Ryan and Bonacursso and report to the crime scene.

By the time the Homicide Detectives were contacted and could get to the scene, it was swarming with reporters, photographers, and a crowd of curiosity seekers as well as numerous nosy police officers and commanders. Detective Sergeant Walker was furious that bystanders and even careless police personnel were trampling the crime scene. He knew that evidence was being destroyed, and Walker immediately cleared the area. While Sergeant Walker, in combination with the other detectives in the homicide squad, examined the crime scene, he ordered that the bodies of the two deceased officers be put in body bags and sent to the city morgue with a uniformed officer in attendance until his detectives could respond.

Chapter Ten

Sergeant John Walker telephoned his commander, Detective Captain James O'Malley, from the East Division Police Station. Walker had been working with and for O'Malley for the past fifteen years. They could read each other as though they were brothers. Both Walker and O'Malley were known throughout the police department as two of the best detectives in the city and had proved it many times over the years. Not only did they have their department's respect, but even the respect of the Federal Bureau of Investigation. Even so, the FBI considered the Kansas City Missouri Police Department one of the most corrupt police agencies in the United States.

O'Malley had attended college in the Midwest, where he obtained a liberal college education. He majored in business and language. His grades were superior to his other classmates. Upon graduation he was offered numerous teaching jobs, but refused all. O'Malley decided instead to enter law enforcement and joined the Kansas City Police Department. O'Malley stood 6'1" and weighed 170 pounds and had dark brown hair and gray eyes. These gray eyes seemed to pierce a person's soul when he looked at you. Many men who were adversaries found his eyes cold and intimidating. As a uniform officer, he found that corruption ran rampant throughout the police force. This was completely controlled by the corrupt city administrations and the gangsters. How he survived as a uniform officer amazed him. But he had the reputation of an honest, sincere, and caring policeman.

After serving three years in uniform patrol, O'Malley was promoted to detective. Here he met John Walker who had also been promoted to detective. These two officers were partnered up and assigned to the Vice Unit for their probation year. They were then assigned to the Burglary Unit and then on to the Homicide Division of the Detective Bureau. By this time they had gained a reputation of being a team that got things done and crimes solved. Criminals feared these two detectives. During O'Malley's eighth year in the department, he was promoted to Detective Sergeant and placed in charge of the downtown Homicide Unit. His first duty was to handpick his own squad, which he did. He took Walker along with him. Those detectives found that he demanded they work hard, and he saw to it that each one was trained in the art of investigation. He also made sure that each officer who worked for him developed skills that would assist them with their investigation. Within this unit O'Malley found himself being promoted to the rank of Lieutenant of Detectives. John Walker was promoted to the squad Sergeant. Both officers had not only been highly decorated within the department, but had become legion in crime fighting. Their solving of homicides made all the force take notice and pride in this team and its unit.

Detective Sergeant Walker, at 5'11" and 220 pounds, was a powerfully built man. His dark brown hair matched his brown eyes. His dress was what one would expect of a detective—cheap suits of a gray or blue material. They were usually wrinkled at the end of the day. Walker always wore white shirts with long sleeves fastened at the cuff with a pair of cuff links his wife gave to him one Christmas after he became a Detective. Walker married his high school sweetheart who gave him eight children. During his early days in the police department, Walker was known as one tough street fighter. Sergeant Walker was an outstanding shot with a revolver. He was recognized as one of the top detective supervisors in the detective divisions, and he was well liked by those he supervised.

Walker hung up the telephone after speaking with his commander and informing him of all the information he had so far. He then phoned the city morgue and asked for Detective Ryan. Soon he was talking to one of his best detectives, Joe Ryan. Ryan had been one of the first detectives picked for Captain O'Malley's squad. Detective Ryan was thirty-eight years old. He was thin and reminded many people of the actor John Garfield. Ryan was extremely handsome and yet tough looking at the same time. He was neat in his appearance as a policeman and highly effective in his job.

"What time is the coroner going to start the autopsies?" asked Walker.

"He informed us he would start as soon as you arrive," answered Ryan.

"Who else is there with you?"

"Bonacursso," replied Ryan.

"Good. Tell the coroner that I will be there in about one hour."

"Will do, boss," stated Ryan.

"And Ryan, do you or Bonacursso need anything from this end?"

"No, boss; we have everything we need."

"Okay; I'll see you soon," replied Walker. Walker hung up the telephone and retrieved all the reports and statements given by the officers and witnesses at the crime scene and headed to the city morgue.

Sergeant Walker entered the morgue with a cup of black coffee and a cigar in his mouth. He greeted his two detectives, Ryan and Bonacursso, and placed his hat and coat on a coat stand in the far corner of the autopsy room. The coroner had not arrived yet, and while waiting the detectives compared their notes from the crime scene. Walker made one statement concerning what he observed at the crime scene. "I have never seen a more fucked up crime scene than what I witnessed when we arrived. And, by God, some of those commanders loitering around the scene acting like rookie cops won't go unnoticed with the Chief."

Bonacursso stated under his breath to Ryan, "Fuck, is he ever pissed!"

Fifteen minutes later the Jackson County Coroner, Dr. James Dooley, arrived and greeted the detectives by name and shook their hands. The detectives and Dr. Dooley had worked closely together on numerous homicides. "Is Captain O'Malley going to be here?" asked Dr. Dooley.

"No," replied Sergeant Walker. "He is with the Chief on other matters."

The doctor then stated that he was waiting for his assistant and then they would start on the autopsy. Detective Bonacursso noticed a third body on another autopsy table and asked, "Who is that corpse?"

"Belongs to a homicide that your boss is working; we are going to autopsy her this afternoon."

As the detectives engaged in small talk with the coroner over freshly brewed cups of hot coffee, Sergeant Walker was looking around the autopsy room. He had to admit that the staff kept a clean, efficient, and orderly room. He observed a sign located in the corner by the staff desk where all the telephones hung. The sign read in Latin, "Hic locus est ubi mori gaudet succussere Vitae," which the Sergeant interpreted to mean, "This is the place where death rejoices to help those who live." Another sign at the cooling room door stated, "You kill them and we will chill them." Dark humor, thought Walker; I guess everyone needs some in this line of work.

A coroner, sometimes referred to as a forensics examiner, is responsible for investigating and determining the cause of death; particularly death that occurs under unusual circumstances. Depending on the jurisdiction, the coroner may adjudge the cause personally or may act as the presiding officer of a special court called a coroner's jury.

Coroners in the United States are usually county-level officers, elected by the vote of the county they serve. In Jackson County, the coroner is a physician. He or she is a specialist in pathology. The autopsy, sometimes called a post-mortem examination, is a systematic, intricate surgical procedure performed after death.

It involves the examination of body tissues and often subsequent laboratory testing to determine cause and manner of death. The body is examined both externally and internally, with examination of all major organs, to document injury or disease. Small samples of internal organs are retained for microscopic examination and body fluids are obtained and tested for drugs and alcohol.

The autopsy procedure is done with respect and seriousness. The prevailing mood in the autopsy room is curiosity, scientific interest, and pleasure at being able to find the truth and share it.

The assistant coroner entered the autopsy room and was greeted by the detectives and Dr. Dooley.

"Walker, are you gentlemen ready to record and photograph this?"

"Yes," stated the detectives.

"Good, then we will proceed," replied the doctor as he motioned all to the first officer's body.

Chapter Eleven

The autopsy room was at fifty degrees, cold enough to cause goose bumps on a living person's skin. Sergeant Walker felt the goose bumps running up his arms and neck. He turned to Detective Joe Ryan and stated, "Joe, you take the photos; and, Phil, you do the recording."

"Yes, sir," stated both detectives at the same time. Both officers had attended many autopsies in the last ten years.

Dr. Dooley checked over all his working tools and started to speak in a loud voice so that all present could hear what was being said. "Today's date is March 8, 1940, at 1300 hours, in the office of the Jackson County Coroner's Office. I am Doctor James Dooley, County Medical Examiner and pathologist for said county. I have in attendance as recorder of record Detective Joseph Ryan, police badge number 103, and Detective Phillip Bonacursso, police badge number 207, who is photographing the events of this autopsy. The supervising detective of this case is Detective Sergeant John Walker, Police Detective Sergeant badge 120. He is also the witnessing investigator of this autopsy. The police case number given this event is KCMO H-150."

"I have before me a Caucasian male who looks to be in his early twenties, brown hair, and hazel eyes. He is clothed in the blue uniform of a Kansas City Missouri patrolman. His uniform and face have what appears to be blood on both. The name tag on his police blouse carries the name of William Toler. A badge number 218 is on the left side of the blouse, identifying that this person is a Kansas City policeman. This person has what appears to be a hole, indicative of a bullet wound, in the middle of his forehead. The Detective Supervisor, John Walker, will assist me with removing the uniform of this person."

The uniform was removed carefully, examined by Walker, and recorded by the assigned detectives. The uniform was then placed in a bag for further examination by the laboratory unit along with his badge number 218 and the officer's name tag. It included one white shirt covered with a dark brown substance thought to be blood, size 15 1/2" neck with a sleeve length of 34". The following items were removed and held as evidence from the body of the officer:

> one black and brown type shoulder strap attached to a
> black leather holster and cuff holder
> one pair of blue wool trousers with a small seam stripe,
> size 29" waist and 33" inseam
> one pair of black heavy soled shoes size ten
> black billfold containing $17.00
> I.D. of William Toler
> one pair of black socks
> one 2" buck folding pocket knife with brown ivory handle
> miscellaneous change of forty-five cents removed from
> pockets of the uniform trousers

"I am now examining the front of the body and only find the one injury in the middle of the forehead with a 2" exit wound to the back of the head. Upon looking over the back of the body I find no other injury except the exit wound, which is leaking brain matter," added Dr. Dooley.

Sergeant Walker now stood back and listened to the pathologist continue speaking as he started his medical examination with scalpel in hand. Walker watched and listened as Dr. Dooley told the detectives to record what he was doing.

"I will now open the body using a Y-shaped incision from the shoulders to mid-chest and down to the pubic region. Next I will open the head," he stated as he made his second incision across the head, joining the bony prominence just below and behind the ears. "When this incision is sewed back up, it will be concealed by the pillow on which the deceased's head rests.

"My incisions are carried down to the skull, then rib cage and breast bone, and then to the cavity that contains the organs of the abdomen. The scalp and the soft tissues in front of the chest are then reflected back where I look around for any abnormalities."

The doctor then looked at the detectives and asked, "Do you detectives know where the word autopsy came from?" Not waiting for an answer, the pathologist continued, "It derives from the ancient Greek autopsia. It means to see for yourself. You see, around 3000 B.C. the ancient Egyptians were one of the first civilizations to practice the removal and examination of the internal organs of humans in the religious practice of mummification."

Dr. Dooley continued to state to his witnesses, "I love to inform students who visit my office to view an autopsy, as well as the new policemen sent to me to observe, just what goes on during the procedure from start to finish. I know that you officers are very familiar with the procedure, but for practice I will narrate what I am doing and why.

"The body is sent to the medical examiner's office by the crime scene detectives in an evidence body bag. A new body bag is used for each body to insure that only evidence from that body is contained within the bag. A sterile sheet is usually wrapped around the body before being put in the body bag. If it is suspected that there may be evidence on the hands, a separate paper sack is put around each hand and taped shut around the wrist.

"There are two parts to the physical examination of the body: the external and internal examination, which includes toxicology and biochemical tests.

"People often ask what is this rubber brick called and what is it for? Well, it is called a body block. It is placed under the back of the body, causing the arms and neck to fall backward while stretching and pushing the chest upward to make it easier to cut open. This gives the pathologist or their assistant maximum exposure to the body trunk. After I have done this, the internal examination begins. The internal examination consists of inspecting the internal organs of the body for evidence of trauma or other indications of the cause of death.

"Just think, detectives; I am giving to you free of charge what has cost me thousands of dollars to learn.

"Gentlemen, I am now opening what is called the pericardial sac so that I may view the heart. Blood for chemical analysis will be removed from the inferior vena cava to the pulmonary veins. Before removing the heart, the pulmonary artery is opened in order to search for a blood clot. I can then remove the heart by cutting the inferior vena cava, the pulmonary veins, the aorta and pulmonary artery, and the superior vena cava. This method leaves the aortic arch intact, which will make things easier for the embalmer. The left lung is then easily accessible and can be removed by cutting the bronchus, artery, and vein at hilum. The right lung can then be similarly removed. The abdominal organs can then be removed one by one after first examining the relationships and vessels.

"Next, the stomach and intestinal contents are examined and weighed. I find this to be useful to find the cause and time of death due to the natural passage of food through the bowel during digestion. The more area empty, the longer the deceased had gone without a meal before death.

"The body block that was used earlier to elevate the chest cavity is removed and used now to elevate the head."

Dr. Dooley then informed the group of detectives that at this point in the autopsy his visitors usually get sick or pass out.

"To examine the brain, I will now make an incision from behind one ear, over the crown of the head, to a point behind the other ear. When I finish this autopsy, I can neatly sew the incision up and it will not be noticed when the head is resting on a pillow in an open casket funeral.

"The scalp is pulled away from the skull in two flaps with the front flap going over the face and the rear flap over the back of the neck. I will then cut the skull with what is called a Stryker saw, named for its manufacturer, to create a 'cap' that can be pulled off to expose the brain. The brain is then observed in situ. Then the brain's connections to the cranial nerves and spinal cord are severed, and the brain is then lifted out of the skull for further examination. If the brain needs to be preserved before being inspected, it is placed in a large container of formalin (fifteen percent solution of formaldehyde gas in buffered water) for at least two, but preferably four, weeks. This not only preserves the brain, but also makes it firmer to allow easier handling without corrupting the tissue.

"An important component of the autopsy is the reconstitution of the body so that it can be viewed, if desired, by relatives of the deceased following this procedure.

"After the examination, the body has an open and empty chest cavity with chest flaps open on both sides. The top of the skull is missing, and the skull flaps are pulled over the face and neck. Normally the internal body cavity is lined with cotton wool or an appropriate material. The organs are then placed into a bag to prevent leakage and returned to the body cavity. The chest flaps are then closed and sewn back together and the skull cap is sewed back in place. The body may then be wrapped in a shroud. The procedure should be undetectable when the deceased is viewed in a funeral parlor after embalming.

"Now that you detectives know everything that I know, let's write up our results and start on the second police officer involved in this unhappy affair."

Chapter Twelve

James Patrick O'Bryan walked into his office with an air of indifference for his staff. There was no "good morning" fanfare with anyone who worked with him. Some, or maybe most, thought O'Bryan was a first-class asshole. O'Bryan was a large, burley, red-faced Irishman. He was as crooked as a figure eight pretzel. He worked intimately with the city's gangsters. He would do anything to turn a dollar. O'Bryan would extort, sell hot merchandise, plan burglaries, robberies, and any other crime he thought would enrich his bank account. He took large cuts from the profits of petty thieves. Jim O'Bryan also leaked information from police cases and secret indictments handed out by the Grand Jury to the gangsters involved for a large profit. If the price was right O'Bryan had no qualms about murder. Along with being a criminal, he was also a Captain in the police department. In fact, he was the police commander of the city jail.

Captain O'Bryan started his police career in 1920 when Tom Pendergast had him appointed to the police department as a foot beat patrolman in the City Market area. Here he quickly learned from the other officers to take a bribe and look the other way when a crime was being committed in his area. The other officers in his station informed him that he should never go home without taking something with him since he didn't make much money working for the city. The profits from crime often paid more in one day than he made in a month. Of course, he had to split his criminal earnings with his supervisor. In turn, his supervisor stayed off his back and allowed free rein in his area of assignment. He was soon involved with the North End gangsters protecting their gambling and prostitution activities. He made himself useful to the underworld as a policeman on the take who could be relied on. They also gave him good information on petty crimes and who committed them so that he could make arrests. He very seldom got a conviction on an arrest, but it made him look good in the eyes of the police higher-ups.

In June of 1933, O'Bryan was working a foot beat patrol at Union Station. On June 17, 1933, he was informed by some underworld associates that he had better make himself scarce as a Federal prisoner was planning to make an escape. This prisoner had been captured in Little Rock, Arkansas, and was being transported by train to Kansas City and on to Leavenworth Penitentiary in Kansas. Somewhere along the way the escape would be made. There would most likely be shooting. He was told that Vern Miller, a local hood, along with Charles Floyd and Adam Richetti would effect the escape. He soon learned that the fugitive was a gangster by the name of Frank Nash. O'Bryan decided to call in sick at the last moment and kept his mouth shut. He did not alert the police department of the impending escape, which led to the murders of four law enforcement officers. O'Bryan was indeed a cold-blooded son of a bitch.

After the escape attempt, which came to be known as the Union Station Massacre, O'Bryan was assigned to chauffer John Lazia. Lazia was Boss Pendergast's right-hand man. He also ran the North End crime family and the Kansas City Police Department. Because of this association Lazia appointed O'Bryan to the rank of Sergeant. After playing politics for his boss, he was appointed to the rank of Lieutenant and transferred to the detective unit. He soon attained the rank of Captain. In this position he had access to information that the underworld needed in order to avoid arrests.

O'Bryan was investigated numerous times for corruption. Nothing ever came of these investigations since most of those who investigated him needed to be investigated themselves. In 1939, O'Bryan realized that a move from city control of the police department to that of state control could prove to be his undoing if he didn't take precautions. He elected to give up his detective status and transferred to the Administration Division where he was put in charge of the city jail. He found that he was able to continue with his criminal occupation.

O'Bryan sat at his desk and answered his telephone after three rings. On the other end of the line was a political boss from the North End Democratic Organization. This was sometimes referred to as the black hand connection. This boss informed him that a "friend of a friend" by the name of Morgan would be contacting him; he needed a favor. The voice went on to state to O'Bryan that it would be well within his position to help. After taking care of the favor he should forget the matter. The caller abruptly hung up. O'Bryan sat in his chair with the telephone receiver in his hand and thought to himself, "Shit, another fucking Dago wanting something. That always means trouble for someone." He hung up the telephone and stated to himself, "I should be able to pick up a few dollars for doing a favor for the North End gang."

A few hours later while the Captain was eating lunch in the detention kitchen, he was notified that he had a call waiting in his office. With a grunt of displeasure at the interruption of his meal, the Captain got up from his table and walked to his office. He closed the office door before picking up the telephone. The caller identified himself as Mr. Morgan and said that he suspected that the Captain had been informed by a mutual friend to expect his call. He had a business proposal to discuss. Mr. Morgan stated to O'Bryan that he would enjoy meeting with him and invited O'Bryan to dine with him at 7:00 p.m. at the Aladdin Hotel supper club. O'Bryan agreed to meet him.

Chapter Thirteen

At the Headquarters building, Captain O'Malley had just finished a meeting with the new Chief of Police and two of the newly appointed Police Commissioners. Both Commissioners had been appointed by the Governor of the State of Missouri. The meeting covered quite a few items, but mainly the death of the two uniformed police officers of the East City Patrol District of Kansas City. It was not a pleasant meeting at all; the department was now catching hell and being pressured from outside political and citizen's groups. There were all types of rumors floating around that the two cops had been on the take, had double-crossed the mob, and were killed for doing so. The newspapers had started the rumors to sell their papers, and it seemed to be working as all the headlines for the last three editions attempted to expound on that rumor. The papers had been selling like hot cakes.

O'Malley now walked from the Chief's Office and headed directly to the Homicide Unit to meet with his detectives to go over the case and the evidence collected. As he walked into the Unit's squad room, he observed Detective Phil Bonacursso working on a very lengthy report. He was typing it up in his hunt and peck manner. It surprised him that Bonacursso was so fast on the typewriter using only two fingers. While approaching Bonacursso, O'Malley observed the red welt scars on the detective's face. He received these scars in a gun battle last year with gangsters from the St. Louis area who had been hired to kill him. During the gunfight Bonacursso had been hit in the right side of his face and chest with a 12-gauge shotgun. Although Bonacursso had returned fire and killed both killers, he had been critically wounded. A year later he was back at his job going full speed. The incident did not affect his job performance in the least. It had taken three serious operations and six months of hard rehabilitation. Bonacursso, according to his supervisor John Walker, had returned to the Homicide Unit with a fearless energy for solving cases and bringing the perpetrators to justice.

O'Malley greeted Bonacursso, asked about his health, and continued into his office just off the squad room. Sergeant Walker was waiting for him.

"Hey, John," greeted O'Malley.

"Back to you, boss," replied the Sergeant. "I bet you were just with the Chief and he was attempting to pressure you about the case setting on your desk."

O'Malley walked to his desk and stared at the file. It was the progressive investigation of the two murdered officers. "I think sometimes that you must be clairvoyant."

"No, James; the grapevine knows all," replied Walker.

O'Malley sat down at his desk and instructed Sergeant Walker to round up his squad and they would review whatever evidence they had on the case.

"Give me fifteen minutes, and I will have them ready," stated Walker.

Walker rounded up the squad and returned to O'Malley's office. The detectives all seated themselves around a long conference table in the center of the room. The Captain looked at his officers and commented, "I expect this case will be on the front page of the papers and lots of pressure will come from the citizens. They will look at these murders and will be asking how the cops can protect them if they can't protect themselves. Our own officers will be asking the same question. I suspect that they will be jumpy and angry over this incident, and they will overreact in many situations in which they find themselves. One more thing, gentlemen; I really need not go into any other reasons for us to solve this homicide other than we have a cop killer out there and I want his ass." O'Malley then picked up the case file in front of him and stated, "Now I want to go over the case step by step to get the proper perspective and grip on this event. Sergeant Walker, let's start on what we know as of this moment."

Walker checked his notes and informed the group that the two murdered police officers were William Toler and Joseph Smith. Officer Toler had been in uniform for two years. Officer Smith was a twenty-eight year veteran of the department.

"I knew Smith," said O'Malley. "He was a drunk and one lazy son-of-a-bitch!"

"Yes, I knew him, too; and I am telling you most police officers wouldn't work with him. He would not have made it much longer under this new Chief," commented Sergeant Walker.

Walker continued from his notes that the two officers had been partners for the past six months and were assigned to the Number Three Patrol Division working the duty tour of 4:00 p.m. to 12:00 a.m. The officers were operating a marked 1941 Ford police vehicle. "According to the activity log of the dispatcher, on the afternoon of the incident the officers were sent to a residence on Third and Van Brunt Boulevard. A report was taken and investigation made at the crime scene. Their next call was an armed robbery that had happened at about 6:00 p.m. where the suspects had already left the scene. A report was taken by the officers and the scene turned over to the District Detectives for investigation. It appears that the officers then took a coffee break at Fifteenth Street and Spruce. Their next call for service was to an unknown type of disturbance a couple of blocks from where they were having coffee. It seems that prior to arriving at the disturbance call they must have become involved in a car check for some unknown reason. We learned this from a witness named Cosgrove who saw a vehicle being chased by the police at St. John Street and Belmont. Our witness stated the vehicle being chased by the officers was a gray Ford, probably a 1936 four-door model. He made reference to the fact that the

Ford had some damage to the front of the car. The witness thought the driver was a white male, but he wouldn't be able to identify the man. After the suspect's vehicle rounded a corner, he lost sight of them. He then heard what he thought were gunshots. The witness continued walking to his place of employment and he observed the police car with its red lights on and the officers laying in the street. He thought that both of the officers were dead. Mr. Cosgrove, our witness, then panicked and ran a couple of blocks where he found a pay phone and called the police station."

Detective Ryan interrupted Walker's recap of the case asking, "Does the witness have a record?"

"No," replied the sergeant. "He is just what he appears to be—a hard working citizen." Walker continued, "I guess that all of the officers who responded to the call of 'assist the officer' forgot everything about protecting the crime scene until our squad got there. Captain, I have never seen a crime scene so fucked up as this one was. The officers tramped all over the scene, as did the commanders who responded. I pointed this out in my crime scene report. I also made a lot of enemies while interviewing the officers and commanders at the scene. Some of these assholes should be demoted or out-and-out fired."

"Perhaps a little retraining in crime scene protection would help in the future," stated O'Malley.

The recap continued with Sergeant Walker informing them that the scene at the site of the murders was handled by Detectives Ryan and Bonacursso. "All witness interviews at the scene, both civilian and law enforcement, were done by Ryan and his partner. Detectives and uniform officers from the Third District did a lengthy area canvas and backtracked to the original call where we suspect the event started," said Walker. "In front of a residence at Third and Bellefontaine we found the dead body of a pimp called Joseph Candanza. His throat had been cut from ear to ear."

"Do we know this guy Candanza?" queried O'Malley.

"Yes," stated Phil Bonacursso. "He works for Torrio, a north end gangster."

"That's right, Phil; I remember him from a couple of homicides we suspected him of doing. He was a Black Hander as I think back," explained Walker. "To continue our recap, Ryan, Bonacursso, and myself responded to the morgue, where the autopsies revealed that Officer Toler was shot in the middle of the forehead, blowing out the back of his head. Officer Smith, it appears, was shot point-blank in the chest three times—killing him instantly."

"Smith was lucky," stated Detective Ryan.

"Why was he lucky?" asked O'Malley.

Detective Ryan responded, "Smith's autopsy revealed that he was dying of cirrhosis of the liver and intestinal cancer. Dying the way he did was much less painful than what he would start feeling in a few months. According to Dr. Dooley he would have been dead in six months anyway."

"We haven't located the getaway car as yet, nor do we have a suspect in mind at this time," Walker informed the Captain. "But we have every informant in the city working and looking for information."

"Well, what we know is that Joseph Candanza was found in the area and murdered by an unknown person who cut his throat. Maybe the two officers, Toler and Smith, came across the event and gave chase to the suspect or suspects and it cost them their lives," O'Malley said in a low voice filled with the sadness that everyone felt.

"Or," replied Walker, "they thought they were chasing a hit-and-run vehicle that collided with a parked car not far from the dead body."

"Food for thought," O'Malley went on to state. "This killing of Candanza might be a gang hit. Put as much pressure as you can on the north end element and their enterprises, and we will see if they would rather tell us something than lose their business. Believe me, someone will talk."

Chapter Fourteen

At seven p.m., O'Bryan was in the lobby of the Aladdin Hotel. He requested that the hotel clerk call Mr. Morgan's room to inform him that his guest had arrived and would be waiting for him in the hotel bar. O'Bryan then walked into the Supper Club Bar, sat down, and ordered a double whiskey on the rocks. He looked around the room and observed little activity and plenty of empty tables. He motioned to the waiter, who was standing at his post in the vestibule of the open room. He requested that he be seated at a table for two in an area of the club where he could conduct a little business without being disturbed. O'Bryan was led to a booth in the rear of the room where he would have privacy. He then instructed the waiter to send his guest, Mr. Morgan, to his table as soon as he appeared. He also informed him that he was Captain O'Bryan. He then slipped the waiter five dollars and thanked him.

The Supper Club band had already set up on the small stage. The feature artist tonight was Artie Shaw, a jazz clarinetist. The music had started with a slow tune unfamiliar to him but very pleasant to the ear. He observed the waiter walking toward him with a man trailing behind. O'Bryan observed that the man was impeccably dressed in a light gray suit. He looked like a college professor, but walked with that self-assured style of a gangster who knows what he wants and how to get it.

Morgan stood at the end of the booth and introduced himself to O'Bryan. O'Bryan suggested that Morgan have a drink prior to eating supper. O'Bryan asked Morgan, "You from Boston or somewhere else in the New England area?"

"You nailed it; I'm from the Boston area," replied Morgan.

"I knew it from your accent. I can always tell—very heavy accent—sounds like you just got off the boat from England," replied O'Bryan.

"And you, Captain, sound like a Midwesterner," stated Morgan.

"Yes, born and raised here in good old Kansas City, Missouri," responded O'Bryan. O'Bryan then pulled two cigars from his vest pocket and offered one to Morgan. Morgan politely refused. O'Bryan lit up his stogie and stated, "Let's you and me get down to business, Morgan. What exactly do you want from me?"

"Since you put it that way, I will be to the point, Captain O'Bryan. I need some information that you can supply for me. I want to know when a certain prisoner in your custody will be picked up by the Army personnel from Fort Leavenworth, Kansas," said Morgan.

O'Bryan asked, "Who is this person who is in my custody?"

"A man by the name of Marcus Kaymark," replied Morgan.

O'Bryan looked at Morgan with a surprised expression on his face, then responded, "Morgan, you must be fucking nuts! Marcus Kaymark is in jail for at least three murders in this city—maybe more. The Army is not interested in him; the Jackson County prosecutor's office wants to try his ass, and they will."

"Captain, I am afraid you are wrong. The Army Intelligence people will take custody of him long before he leaves your jail."

"Why is that?" asked O'Bryan.

"Simple, my friend; they think he is a spy of some sort who might have information they want," replied Morgan.

"Hell, if he might be a spy why do you want the information about when the Army is taking him?" asked O'Bryan.

"I really think it is better that you don't know any more than what I have just told you. It might not be in your best interest.

Besides, I was told by a mutual friend that you could be relied on. Was he wrong?"

"No, not at all. If the Army picks him up I will be notified and I will notify you. However, I am taking a chance of someone finding out that it was me tipping you."

Peter Morgan pulled a white envelope from the breast pocket of his suit jacket and handed it to the Captain. "I don't expect you to work for free, and I do expect you to keep your mouth shut. Our mutual friend said you were a stand-up man and could be trusted completely. You will find three thousand dollars in the envelope. Do we have an arrangement?"

O'Bryan looked into the envelope while thumbing the cash. "Yes, we have a deal."

"Good; I expect that you will know in the next few days when the Army will pick the prisoner up. If you should feel patriotic for some reason and decide to shortchange me, our mutual friend told me to tell you that your career will end."

"Shit, Peter; I wouldn't double-cross you; my word is my bond."

"Wonderful, Captain; now let's order and have a pleasant supper and enjoy each other's conversation. Oh, by the way Captain, you can contact me by phone here at the hotel. If I don't answer just leave a message at the desk. I will get it."

After their dinner and a few more drinks, Morgan dismissed himself from the table. He informed O'Bryan that he had a meeting with another person at 10:00 p.m. in his room. Morgan called the waiter and instructed him to put the dinner and drinks on his tab and all the extra drinks the Captain wanted during the evening. He then shook O'Bryan's hand, wished him a good evening, and left the restaurant.

O'Bryan ordered another drink and thought to himself that there was a lot more to this than an escape, if indeed his guess was correct and this Morgan or some other person was planning an escape for Kaymark. One thing that bothered him was that the Kaymark case belonged to Captain James O'Malley's squad, and O'Malley was one person that O'Bryan didn't want looking into him or his activities. He knew that O'Malley already suspected him of being on the take from previous investigations involving corruption charges. It was well known that O'Bryan was mobbed up. No way was he going to take a chance like this for only three grand. He would have to have at least ten grand for putting his neck out. As O'Bryan got more intoxicated, he decided to tell Morgan that he would have to come up with seven thousand more in cash for him to take the chance.

After four more drinks to build his courage, O'Bryan found himself in front of Morgan's room door. He knocked hard and loud on the door, and Morgan answered shortly. He invited O'Bryan in. As O'Bryan stepped in, he looked around the room. He realized that a room like this probably cost two hundred fifty dollars a night.

Morgan broke the silence between them. "What do you want, Captain O'Bryan?" The tone in his voice should have alerted the captain not to push, but the booze he had put away made his normal caution take flight.

O'Bryan said, "I was thinking our deal over, pal; and I'm thinking that I need ten grand to expose myself to future problems by giving you the information on Mr. Kaymark. Besides, if the Army wants him in their custody and the prosecutor is willing to let him go with them, then I figure that there must be a bigger reason that they are letting him go. I think if the prosecutors aren't making a fuss, then Kaymark must be going to testify against someone who is willing to compensate me more money for the chances I am taking in giving you the information that you want."

"You mean to extort more money after we had a deal, Captain? You know, I don't think that would be smart," intoned Morgan with a stare that locked with O'Bryan's eyes.

"Fuck you, tough guy with your bad ass stare. It don't scare me one bit. If you want the information, give me the money I want."

Morgan's face flushed bright red as he looked at the cop shaking him down for more money. "Okay, my friend, but I only have two thousand more to give you. If that isn't enough then give me back the money I gave you. You aren't getting any more from me."

The cop looked at Morgan with the tipsy stare of an intoxicated man while he was deciding whether or not to insist on the ten grand or the two thousand more that was being offered.

"I'll take it," said O'Bryan.

Morgan removed a roll of money from his pocket, counted out two thousand dollars, and handed it to the Captain.

The cop, thinking he could do no better, stated," I'll let you know the time as soon as I know." He then headed to the door and exited with his money and a grin on his face.

Zino Torrio stepped out of the bedroom with a cigar in his mouth.

"Did you hear all that shit?" asked Morgan.

"Yes; I think he is too greedy for his health," replied Torrio.

"Do I need to worry about the Captain?"

"No, he will be taken care of before he can cause you or me any trouble," stated Torrio.

Chapter Fifteen

O'Malley dismissed his detectives and allowed Sergeant Walker to supervise the squad's activity concerning the homicide of the two police officers. O'Malley remained in his office answering the telephone. He had received calls from numerous off-duty police officers who wanted to come in and work without pay to assist with the investigation. O'Malley assured them of his heartfelt thanks and pride in those officers who were volunteering their time and energy. The Captain took their names and told each that Sergeant Walker would contact them if help were needed.

The Chief of Police telephoned O'Malley to inform him that he had a press conference at 1:30 p.m. this day. He wanted O'Malley there with him to handle most of the questions that the press might ask.

Detective Bonacursso, along with his partner Joe Ryan, was revisiting the crime scene, hoping to find something that had been overlooked. They parked their unmarked police unit at the exact location where the two murdered officers had stopped their vehicle. Both detectives walked the road and shoulder area of the scene with negative results. They then decided to backtrack the car chase route. The detectives canvassed the chase area on foot with no positive information or clues to add to the investigation. They did discover that the east patrol detectives had made a most efficient canvas. The east zone detectives had developed the area where it was suspected the car chase began. The two officers of the homicide unit returned to their police vehicle and drove to the east patrol division to talk to their detectives, read the area canvas, and look over written reports.

Detective Bonacursso interviewed most of the detectives while Ryan read over all of their written reports at the police station. Two of the detectives interviewed by Bonacursso were personal friends of his. This friendship made it much easier for the information they had gathered to flow cop to cop—both what had been included in the reports and the information that had been held back because of leaks within the Division. Both of the detectives that Bonacursso talked to were of Italian descent and familiar with most of the gangsters, mobbed up or not. Both officers believed that the crime was associated with prostitution and gambling. They also thought that the man found dead at the scene of the earlier disturbance responded to by the two murdered officers was killed by whoever murdered the police officers.

Both east zone detectives knew the gangster Joseph Candanza and suspected his association with the mob boss, Zino Torrio. The officers informed Bonacursso that Torrio was aware of almost every crime in the city and that he got a kickback on nearly every crime committed in the area. Both detectives had heard from their sources that Torrio had put a contract out on Candanza for holding out on his cut of the ill-gained monies from Candanza's gambling and prostitution activities. They had not heard yet from their informants who the killer or killers were. If they had to guess who the killer or killers might be, they would suspect one or more of at least five stone cold killers used by the mob in Kansas City. Their guess was Phil Simone, Vic Gargotta, Anthony Gizzo, Gus Bruno, or Sal DeMarko. Any of these killers could be involved. It could also be someone brought in from the outside for this particular job.

As Ryan and Bonacursso walked out of the third district station house, they looked at each other. Bonacursso stated, "Joe, I think it's nothing more than a mob hit, and our murdered officers just happened to see something and gave chase to the killer or killers without knowing what had gone down. The killer caught them off guard."

Ryan totally agreed, stating," It's going to be a bitch to get anyone to talk!"

Chapter Sixteen

O'Malley met with the Chief at 1:00 p.m. and gave the Chief most of the information concerning this case.

"Shit, how much of this case should we let the press have?" asked the Chief.

"Only what we suspect happened and nothing else; anything more would hurt our attempts to solve the case," replied the Captain. "You know the press—unless we give them something to get their teeth into they will make up their own story or what they have heard from leaks in the department and embellish what they want in order to make a story. If you think that will work, let's go and meet the press." The Chief and O'Malley walked out of his office and into the press room next door to the Chief's office.

After about an hour of fielding questions from the press, the Chief ended the press conference, assuring the news people of the department's complete cooperation as the case developed. He also assured the general public that this was most likely a gangster hit that should not be thought of as anything else. The killing of the two officers apparently was related to the homicide of a north end gangster and the officers were shot pursuing the suspect or suspects. He expected an arrest in a matter of days.

After returning to his office with O'Malley and the Chief of Detectives, the Chief informed them that he had put the crime solving detectives on the spot in the press conference. They had better solve the damn thing quick!

O'Malley returned to his own office where he again met with his operation sergeant Walker and reviewed all pending murder cases under investigation. They both worked late into the night. Around 9:00 p.m., Detective Ryan walked into the Homicide Office and asked if either O'Malley or Walker had read the evening paper. Both replied that they had not.

Ryan handed the paper to Sergeant Walker, who then read the headlines.

"Chief of Police and his detectives have no real clue as to who killed two of their officers."

"Shit," Walker stated, "the fucking newspaper is attempting to sell more papers. It goes on to state that the Chief is warning the top police supervisor of the Homicide Unit and the Chief of Detectives to get the crimes solved."

"John, we knew the pressure would head our way on this; and the Chief, being new, is just covering his ass."

"Jim," Walker continued, "the shithead who wrote this article is also stating that while all the detectives are working on the cop murders they are neglecting the other homicides that have happened. Hell, he has quoted you from your bio as stating that detectives as well as the uniform police officers have a wide variety of techniques available in conducting investigations. However, the majority of cases are solved by the interrogation of suspects and interviewing of witnesses, which takes lots of time. Sometimes detectives may rely on a network of informants which has been cultivated over the years. Often informants have connections with individuals a detective would not be able to approach formally. So many times cases, especially homicide cases, are solved with the information supplied by informants and the evidence collection and its preservation by other members of the police department. If this is true and there seems to be no real clues, can this crime be solved?"

"What an asshole," remarked Ryan. He continued reading the article for the other two men's information. "It seems the case will rest with a Detective Captain by the name of James O'Malley, who is a twenty-eight year veteran of this police department. Captain O'Malley has served throughout the ranks as a police officer, sergeant, lieutenant, and captain. As a police executive, he has been the commander of the Homicide Unit for the past fifteen years. He graduated cum laude from City College. He has instructed at the police academy. O'Malley has had dozens of articles on police techniques in criminal cases and two instructional books on homicide investigations which are used in most major police departments. He has handled more than four hundred murder cases as a detective and supervisor. This Captain is the recipient of over sixty awards for bravery and exceptional work. He is a man who believes in continuous training and education for all police officers. His detectives are handpicked and are considered the cream of the crop within the detective division. Let's now see if he and his detectives can live up to this crime challenge."

"Boy, boss; it sounds like our Detective Chief put it all on you," stated Walker.

"Well, fellows; it's up to us," replied O'Malley.

"Are all our men signed out for the night?" asked O'Malley.

"Yes," replied Walker.

"Who is handling the dog watch shift?"

"Detective Croix has the duty," replied Walker.

"Let's call it a night," stated the Captain.

Chapter Seventeen

Captain O'Malley reported in very early at the headquarter building. He was smartly dressed in a black suit, white shirt, and light gray tie. His shoes where black and highly shined. He had attended the early viewing of the murdered police officers. The funeral would be attended by more than half of the Police Department personnel, dignitaries of the city, and many outside police agencies showing their respect for the fallen officers. The funeral and parade would be remembered for years to come.

O'Malley had received a call from a confidential informant who thought he might have some information that would help in a murder case. He was to meet the informant on the south side of the city at a real estate office parking lot. They were to meet at 11:00 a.m.

O'Malley picked up the homicide book so far developed on the police officers. He sat down at his desk and started reading. After he finished the reports, he was interested in the new reports written by Detectives Bonacursso and Ryan, where they had mentioned their interview with the third district detectives. There they had mentioned five possible men capable of the type of killings performed on the gangster Candanza and the two officers. He was aware of Sal DeMarko, Gus Bruno, and Anthony Gizzo. They were the older enforcers of the mob, and he had arrested all of them at one time or another. He had no personal information on Gargotta, and though he had heard of Phil Simone, he knew nothing further.

O'Malley found himself walking to the police records unit where he had the clerk pull the file jackets on all five of the gangsters. Upon looking through the files he realized that most of the records had been purged from the files. Most of the information concerning their arrests and convictions was missing. O'Malley knew that the older gangsters, years ago, had the power and influence to get the files purged. He made a mental note to check with the Federal Bureau of Investigation and see what information they had on the five.

At 10:45 a.m., O'Malley was waiting in the parking lot of the real estate company. He observed a green 1938 Plymouth pull into the lot and drive towards his vehicle. The driver of the Plymouth pulled in next to O'Malley's' vehicle. O'Malley motioned for him to get into his unmarked police car. The confidential informant was a heavyset, dark complected negro in his mid-sixties. He was the owner of numerous black saloons, a well-known gambler, and a brothel owner. He was known to work closely with the Italian mobsters as well as other white and black gangsters of the city. O'Malley knew the black criminal well and had used him on numerous cases. His information was always on the mark. He also had heard that some of the come lately gangsters were trying to take over his criminal enterprises. He had also heard on the street that a couple of city politicians were attempting to back those Turks attempting to move in on his territory.

The black gangster shook hands with O'Malley, "Long time; no see, Captain."

"Yes, its' been awhile. What have you got in the way of information, and what do you want in return?"

"God damn, O'Malley, always to the point. No time to socialize for awhile?"

"I have known you for twenty years and I am still not your friend, Jonas," stated O'Malley.

"I know, I know, with us it's just business. So I'll just tell you, Jim; I got a problem and you've got a problem, and I think we can help each other."

"I am listening."

"My problem is those goddamned punk ass, mother fucking nigger hoodlums and the city politicians are trying to put me out of the money!" As Jonas Carter spoke, spittle ran down his jaw. "But, Jim, you got a problem, too, with a bunch of unsolved murders and some you don't know about yet!"

"What makes you think that I can help you out with your problems?" asked O'Malley.

"Simple, Captain, you have helped me before when some of those Dago mugs tried to muscle me out of business. I know you're one of the honest coppers in the business. I also know if you want to you can put their crooked asses in jail. Shit, boss, they have been taking bribes for years and buying votes from the colored members of the city to stay in office. I can help you put them in jail. Hell, I will not only get enough people who take the bribes to testify for you, but I will, too."

"I'll tell you what, Jonas Carter. You give me something good that we can get our teeth into first, then I'll work with you on your problem. But it will have to be good."

"How about I tell you the name of a lowlife who rapes and kills women!"

"What murder are you talking about, Jonas?"

"The woman killed in the Brookside area."

"You're talking about the nurse?"

"Yes," replied Carter.

"A guy by the name of Leon Booker, lives over by where the nurse worked."

"How do you know?"

"Well, boss, I didn't see him do it, but he has been bragging about raping and killing a white woman the other day."

O'Malley thought for a few seconds before answering him. "O.K., Jonas, if you are correct on this I will look into your problems."

"It's good, boss; it's good information."

The Captain looked at the informant with cold steely eyes as he asked his next question, "Do you know anything about the murder of the two police officers?"

"No, but I will ask around for you."

"Jonas, have you ever had dealings with a guy by the name of Phil Simone?"

O'Malley observed that Jonas actually turned gray and avoided O'Malley's eyes. He then became nervous and stuttered as he started to talk.

"N-nno, I don't do business with him."

"That's not what I asked you. Do you know him?"

"Yes, he is a north end gangster."

"How about Vic Gargotta?"

"No," replied Carter. "I don't know nothing about him."

"Anthony Gizzo or Gus Bruno or maybe Sal DeMarko?"

"I know who all of them are and who they work for, they are big league hitters you don't want to know much about."

O'Malley felt sure that for some reason Jonas was keeping something back from him concerning those five names, but for now he would not press it.

"O.K., Jonas, I will let you know what kind of deal we have if your information turns out."

O'Malley shook hands again with his confidential informant and watched him step into his Plymouth and drive out of the lot. O'Malley sat a few moments longer in the lot and thought about what he had learned. His thoughts went back to the five names he had asked Jonas about. He pulled out his notebook from his breast pocket and wrote the names down along with a reminder to contact the FBI. He then put his vehicle in gear and drove out of the parking lot and headed for his unit. He would give the information provided by his confidential informant to Sergeant Walker and let him follow up as it was his case.

Chapter Eighteen

arly that afternoon, O'Malley was summoned again to the Office of the Chief of Police, where not only the Chief was seated at a conference table, but also the Chief of Detectives and a man approximately O'Malley's age. This unknown man was dressed in the uniform of an Army officer supporting the rank of a full bird colonel. As O'Malley entered the office, all three of the men rose to greet him.

The Chief introduced the uniformed officer as Colonel Tom Small, a colonel in the Army Intelligence Division assigned to the Anti-Terrorist Division out of Washington, D.C. The colonel approached O'Malley with his hand out and gave O'Malley a hardy handshake. He stated, "I am very happy to meet you, Captain O'Malley. Your Chief of Police and Detective Chief have had only the best things to say about you and your squad."

"Thank you, Colonel Small; it's always nice to hear a compliment concerning your work and the outstanding people working for you." The Chief then pointed to a chair and ordered O'Malley to pull it up to the table along with the other men. Chief of Detectives John Miller walked to the office door and contacted the officer on duty there and stated, "We want no disturbance while this door is closed. Do you understand?"

"Yes, sir," replied the officer as the Detective Chief closed the door.

The Chief then informed O'Malley that Colonel Small had requested this meeting and that it concerns one of our investigations. I will let the Colonel explain what he needs and why he called the meeting."

Colonel Small pulled open a brown leather briefcase and retrieved a file, opened it, and after a short pause, looked at O'Malley and said, "I am interested in a case involving a man named Marcus Kaymark."

"Kaymark, as in the person we have arrested for several murders here in Kansas City?" asked O'Malley.

"Yes, that's the man."

"You know, Colonel, we also suspect he has been involved in several other suspicious deaths."

"Yes, I have read the file and investigation on him. Captain O'Malley, I will get to the point. Kaymark is a German spy. We have learned of his long history in espionage and sabotage in other countries throughout the European area; we definitely want him in our custody. I want you to know that without the alertness of your detectives when they arrested him and recovered suspicious papers, we would not know about his long involvement in the world of espionage. Your officers contacted our office with the information they had and we sent a crew of Military Police investigators who recovered papers and equipment that only a spy would have use for. We think Kaymark, which isn't his real name, had illegally entered the United States through Mexico along with a couple of other spies we are just learning about. We have also learned that he has been involved in quite a few attempts at sabotage on the east coast. I can tell you for certain that we will make him talk and turn him to our way of thinking."

O'Malley nodded and then asked, "What about the murders he has committed?"

"Unfortunately, he will not be tried for them, but released to the Army. I can assure you that he will never get out of our stockade, but he doesn't need to know that."

"Then I guess you and the Army have got a new prisoner. My detectives, especially the ones that worked the case, won't be happy about not seeing the son of a bitch die at Jefferson City. But I am sure they will enjoy knowing that he will never see the light of day, and I guess it will make them happy that a spy was caught."

"I am sorry, Captain, but you cannot mention the fact that he is a spy to anyone—not even your own people. Only we four will know about this. No one else in the department is to know," stated the Colonel in a very serious voice.

"I understand," replied O'Malley.

"If it is any consolation to you, O'Malley, we have already made several arrests of agent provocateurs as well as sleeper agents as a result of your detectives' information on this guy. They will all be prosecuted under the 1917 Espionage Act, which will result in many executions if and when they are convicted by the Federal Courts. However, Captain, we will do our best to turn some of these spies to work for us. We all know that it is only a matter of time before we are forced into the war in Europe, and we had better be prepared. If we are not, a spy could cause us to be highly injured here at home."

"Sounds to me, Colonel Small, that you guys know what you are doing; but I feel like we should be privy to any criminal cases those people you are arresting have been involved in so that they can be cleared from the police books," replied O'Malley.

"That is only fair, Captain, and it will be done. But only if it doesn't involve or hurt National Security."

"When are you taking custody of Kaymark?" asked the Chief of Detectives.

"That information will be relayed to the Chief only when the time comes. Remember the fewer who know that information the better."

"Fair enough," stated the detective chief.

As the meeting broke up, Colonel Small thanked O'Malley for his cooperation in this matter and assured him of all cooperation if and when O'Malley ever needed it.

Captain O'Bryan found himself actually working for a change in his office, going over the incoming activity reports. This was usually handled by his Operations Sergeant. However, it was his day off and the captain didn't trust anyone else to do them. So here he was reading the shit as it came in over his teletype and making notations. His desk clerk entered his office with some new memorandums and release information. Suddenly he spotted an interesting memo from the Chief of Police indicating that one Marcus Kaymark would be released to the custody of the Military Police on March 10, 1940. Today's date was March 8. He then contacted his outside clerk and told him he was going to the first floor to talk to another person. O'Bryan walked down the stairs to the first floor where he exited to the street and walked to a pay phone booth. He pulled a coin out of his pocket and started to drop it in, but instead he hesitated and thought that he really ought to try and get more money out of this bastard Morgan. He then disregarded the thought and dialed the number of the Aladdin Hotel where he asked for Morgan's room. After a few rings the phone was answered by Morgan. The Captain asked, "Do you recognize my voice?"

"Yes, I do."

"March 10th at 0600 hours." The Captain then hung up the phone and returned to his office.

Chapter Nineteen

O'Malley was in his office early the next day. He hadn't slept well and although he was clean shaven and dressed in a freshly cleaned gray suit and white shirt, he felt tired and sluggish. He skipped eating breakfast and held a cup of black coffee in his hand that he had picked up at the local greasy spoon. He was standing looking out of the office window when Operations Sergeant Walker arrived. O'Malley turned and looked at him and nodded in greeting as did Walker. O'Malley moved in front of Walker and in a low voice informed him of the conversation he had in the Chief's office the night before.

"John, I'm violating the Chief's order not to speak about this matter to anyone; but I feel you are entitled as my second in command of this unit and working supervisor of the Kaymark case to know."

"Shit, Jim, I'll have to say something to the detectives that worked the case or they will wonder why there is no prosecution on the asshole." O'Malley thought about whether to include the detectives in on the information or not. He then informed Walker to reach out for the detectives involved in the case and have them in his office at 0900 hours. He would advise the officers himself. O'Malley then sat down at his desk and approved the reports from the night shift.

He then picked up the newspaper and read the continuous bullshit written on the case of the murdered police officers.

At 0900 hours O'Malley found himself facing the two detectives, Ryan and his partner Bonacursso. He had them close the door to his office so no one else could hear what he was about to tell them.

"I called you two here so that I could share some information with you concerning the Kaymark case."

"Something wrong with the investigation?" asked Ryan.

"No, you two detectives did an outstanding job on that case. In fact the chief is writing you two an accommodation for the job you did with the case. Shit, guys, the only problem with the case is that the United States government is going to take custody of Mr. Kaymark for other reasons and his prosecution will have to wait. There is nothing more I can share with you about the reason for this except it is a confidential matter not to be discussed outside of this room."

"I understand, Captain," stated Ryan. Bonacursso shook his head in agreement.

"Good, now we have a cop killer to find," replied Sergeant Walker who was standing in a corner of the office and had not been seen by the two detectives. Both O'Malley and Walker dismissed the two policemen to continue their investigation.

Bonacursso and Ryan left the squad room and drove to the local hangouts in an attempt to locate any of the five gangsters thought to be involved in the police murders. The two cops started with all the known bars and joints where each one of the gangsters hung out. They left their calling cards with every bar owner whom they had contact with. After several hours on the street looking for the mobsters, both officers returned to their office and started writing their reports which indicated nothing more than a lot of negative results.

Ryan, as senior detective, told Bonacursso to finish up his report and they would call it a day as soon as he reported their search results to Sergeant Walker. Ryan entered his supervisor's office and observed him going over reports that other squad members had turned in.

"Say, Sarge; Phil and I didn't have much luck in finding any of the five thugs we're looking for in any of their usual haunts."

"Joe, do you think they might be ducking you?"

"No idea, Sergeant; most generally they are easy to find. We've put the word out all over town that we want to talk to them. Every beat cop and vice detective have their eyes open. Hell, we even contacted some of the newspaper men to let them know that we want to talk to those five. I even told them we would give them a scoop if one of them found out where they were."

"O.K., Ryan, as soon as Phil turns in the reports for O'Malley to read, go on home and enjoy the rest of the evening. You both look beat."

Ryan walked out of the office and into the squad room. "I am just about finished with our write up, Joe."

"Good, let's get the fuck out of here and go home."

At 10:30 p.m., an alert foot beat patrolmen spotted Anthony Gizzo in a strip bar on Eighth Street and Broadway. The Officer took Gizzo into custody for investigation on the information he had obtained from the homicide detectives. He was transported to the city jail, where the detectives would question him in the morning. Gizzo, at the time of his apprehension, was too intoxicated to resist.

As luck would have it, another mobster, Sal DeMarko, was spotted at Thirty-First and Main by a vice detective. He and his partner observed DeMarko selling what appeared to be drugs to a couple of users. Both vice cops walked toward DeMarko. As they did, DeMarko spotted them and the foot chase was on. DeMarko ran into the hallway of an apartment building. As he ran, he started dropping the contraband he was carrying. He then ran out of the building's back door and onto the street. As he hit the street, DeMarko lost his footing and fell flat on his face. While he attempted to recover from his embarrassment, both of the detectives jumped on him and gave the dope dealer a royal ass kicking, especially after a .45 caliber Colt automatic pistol was located in his waistband.

DeMarko, after being stitched up at the hospital, was transported to the city jail for investigation in connection with the murder of the two police officers and possession and sale of heroin. They also threw in resisting arrest and carrying a concealed weapon, which the police files showed to have been stolen in a residential burglary.

The following morning Captain O'Malley entered his office, grabbed a cup of black station coffee, seated himself at his desk, and started looking over the reports on his desk. He noticed the two arrest reports of the mobsters and immediately had Gizzo rousted out of his intoxicated slumber and brought to the detectives' holding cells where he took a good hard look at him. Gizzo was a large fat man in his early forties. He had balding brown hair and a large mustachio. At 5'7", he sure didn't look like a cold blooded killer, especially as he had pissed his trousers and smelled so bad from the booze scent that it almost made O'Malley gag. He watched the gangster, who was still intoxicated, laying on the floor where he had passed out. While Gizzo was passed out, he vomited all over the cell. O'Malley then returned to his office, called the detention unit, and ordered Gizzo returned to a cell up there until he sobered up.

Sergeant Walker walked into the office ready for the day's work. O'Malley brought him up to date on the arrests and their conditions. It was decided that the Captain and Walker, due to the fact that they both knew these two thugs and had arrested them several times in the past, would interrogate both later in the day. In the mean time, they would have the other detectives continue looking for the other three as soon as they reported to work. This just might be the day the detectives would get a break in their case.

Chapter Twenty

O'Malley and his operations sergeant had their lunch together at a cafeteria on Grand Ave. Upon finishing their meal and sipping their second cup of coffee, O'Malley stated, "John, I have some information supplied by an informant we have both used in the past by the name of Jonas Carter."

"I remember him, Jim; he helped us on a couple of cases. His information always turned out to be right on the mark."

"Yes, that is the man. He wants to trade information on one of the homicides you caught in the Brookside area."

"You mean the nurse?"

"Yes."

"What does he have to say on it?"

"Carter said he had heard that a fellow by the name of Leon Booker, who resides over by the hospital where the nurse was employed, has been bragging to people that he did it."

"I've never heard his name before," stated Walker.

"I checked on his record and found that he has been arrested for rape, aggravated assault, and gambling. He is known to be handy with a knife."

"Jim, I don't need to tell you that we have very little to go on at this point and the investigation is really at a standstill with everything else we have on our plate at this time. We do know that most of the furniture in the victim's apartment appeared to be new. I was going to run that clue down when the officers were killed and became the priority of the department. I will be more than happy to snatch Mr. Booker up for questioning."

"Good, John; it's up to you. But I would like for you to assign Detective Robert Croix and the two detectives from the Third Division to apprehend Booker. Croix needs the experience, and it's good politics to use the Third District as they have been working overtime on the murder of the police officers."

"I agree with you on that score," replied Walker.

"Tell me, Captain, what kind of trade did Carter want?"

"Simple, his turf is being invaded by young Turks and a couple of city politicians. He states he can get some voters who sold their votes to certain politicians and they will give us statements for the record. They are willing to testify against the two that have aligned themselves with the young Turks who want him out of the way. We will see what we can do only after his information has been verified with an arrest and conviction."

"I'll get on this as soon as I return to the office," stated the sergeant.

Sergeant Walker telephoned Detective Robert Croix at his home and instructed him to respond to his office for an assignment. Walker then phoned Detective Sergeant Mills Franchier of the Third Division Detective Unit and advised him that he was going to arrest a murder suspect who lived in their area, and he was requesting assistance with the apprehension and what detectives he wanted on the arrest. Sergeant Franchier agreed to assisting and would have the detectives waiting for him at the Third Division Detective Office.

When Detective Croix responded to Walker's office, he was advised of the case and the information that had been learned from the informant. Walker left Croix with the murder book to review while Walker walked downstairs from the Headquarter building to the Police Record Bureau where he pulled Leon Booker's criminal jacket along with the latest mug shot of him and reviewed his record. Leon Booker, according to his file, had served penitentiary time in Jefferson City, Missouri, for robbery, assault, rape and gambling.

His file also indicated that he had numerous arrests in the past for bootlegging. The rape charge was entered by arrest in 1919; he had served ten years for all those charges. He was not known to carry a firearm, but was listed as being very handy with a knife. He was left-handed, five feet nine inches tall, and weighed one hundred sixty-five pounds. He was in extremely good shape.

As Walker looked at Booker's mug shot, he noticed that he was starting to bald and had what hair he had left cut short to his head. The file indicated that he worked for a moving company as contractor. According to the update on his file, he owned his own moving van. Since getting out of prison Booker had been arrested for investigation in connection with four different rapes. There seemed never to be enough evidence to convict. Either the victims refused to prosecute or they recanted their stories. Booker's latest address was 907 Paseo Boulevard, apartment #7, and it appeared that he has lived there for the past five years.

Armed with the file information, Walker verified by phone book that Booker still resided at the location indicated in the file. He and Detective Croix then met with the Third Division Detectives and went over the case and everything known about the suspect Booker. They decided to attempt Booker's arrest around 10:00 p.m. at his residence.

The detectives would travel in two separate vehicles. Sergeant Walker would be armed with a sawed off 12 gauge shotgun, and the three detectives armed with their service revolvers. The arresting detectives would be the Third Division officers with Croix and Walker as the backups. The suspect would be taken to the Third Division for booking and interrogation of his involvement in this murder.

At 10:30 p.m., all four officers entered the suspect's apartment after Detective Croix obtained a pass key from the building super for Booker's pad. They found the apartment to be unoccupied. Sergeant Walker decided that they would wait for the suspect. At 11:45 p.m., Leon Booker entered his apartment and was immediately apprehended without incident.

After Leon was booked in at the Third Division Station and locked in a holding cell, the four detectives discussed the crime scene of the murder and decided the Third Division Detectives would start the interrogation in an attempt to get a confession. If they were unsuccessful then Walker and Croix would take the interrogation over.

At 3:00 a.m., Leon Booker confessed to the murder of Ms. Paula Liston as well as numerous other rapes he had committed in the last two years. Booker told the officers in the course of his confession that he had seen the woman for the first time while he was being treated for a foot injury at St. Joseph Hospital. He then saw her again at Murphy's Department Store where he worked as a delivery contractor. He noticed that she had purchased a new bed, mattress, and sofa. He made sure that he got the delivery items to her apartment in the Plaza area of the city. Upon his delivery of the nurse's furniture, Booker was admitted to her apartment where he carried the furniture and helped her arrange the furniture. While in her bedroom setting up her bed and new mattress, he made up his mind that he was going to rape this white woman. She was so friendly he thought that she wanted him as much as he wanted her. Her small, well developed body turned him on and he found himself with a hard-on that actually hurt. All he could think of was fucking her hard and fast.

He watched as the woman put on a bed sheet and blanket. She had turned her back on him and continued messing with the covers. At that time he grabbed her around the neck. She started screaming and struggling. He was amazed by her strength and chocked her with his arm even harder. Leon snatched a pair of stockings from her dresser top and forced them into the woman's mouth, muffling her screams and yells for help. He had her face down on her stomach with him on her back. Booker then removed a red tie from around his neck and knotted the tie around her throat. He then ripped most of her clothes off and had sex with her on her new mattress. While he was having intercourse with the woman from the rear, Booker got so excited that he tightened the tie without realizing it. He soon realized she wasn't fighting any longer and he continued having sex with her. When he turned her over to enter her from the front he discovered that she was dead. However, this didn't stop him from having intercourse with her. He then found that she had scratched several areas of his face. This so enraged Leon that he picked the woman up from the bed and threw her to the floor on the other side of the bed. He then pulled the mattress over the woman's body. He composed himself and looked around the room for money, located her purse and removed $25.00 and some change. He then exited her apartment and continued with his deliveries within the city.

Sergeant Walker told the Third Division cops to remove the suspect Booker to the city jail. Then they were to finish up their reports and give them to him for review before they took Booker to the prosecutor's office for arraignment. Walker then called his boss, James O'Malley, and filled him in on all the events of the arrest and confession.

Later that afternoon, O'Malley had Leon Booker brought to the HQ Homicide Office for questioning. While questioning Leon, O'Malley listened closely as the suspect repeated his confession. As Booker concluded his narrative, O'Malley asked him whether there was any little detail he might have overlooked when he gave his statement to the detectives.

"Yes, the bitch was on the rag."

Now there was no doubt that Booker had killed the woman. He ordered Booker to be taken back to his cell.

Chapter Twenty-one

Detective Robert Croix graduated from college at twenty-three years of age with a degree in business and accounting. He was very fortunate that his parents had made their fortune in the meat packing business during the early 1900s in Kansas City and Chicago. At both cities they had built a mighty empire in the slaughter houses and meat packing industry. Robert's father expected his youngest son to join his five brothers in the family business. Robert was sent to the finest schools and college. His grades were very good, but his father learned early that his son was an adventuresome individual and showed no desire to enter the family business. Instead, Robert informed his father that he didn't mind the stink of the stock yards nor the smell of the slaughter houses, but he just wasn't interested in working in the family business at this time in his life. He stated that he needed excitement in his choice of jobs and wanted to serve his fellow man. He was going to enter law enforcement. In fact, he told them that he wanted to work for the Kansas City Police Department and wanted no interference whatsoever from his family.

Shortly thereafter, Robert applied to the Police Department of Kansas City and had been accepted as a patrolman. He was sent to the police academy for his law enforcement training. Robert Croix stood five foot, ten inches tall in his stocking feet and weighed one hundred sixty pounds. He had a well muscled body, dark brown hair, and hazel eyes. He was considered to be a handsome man with an easygoing manner. Upon completing the police training, he was assigned to the downtown patrol division on foot patrol. Shortly after, he was noticed by his supervisors and commanding officer as an outstanding police officer. His arrests were quality, his reports outstanding, and he was a team leader at crime scenes. He was noticed by the district detectives who worked with him. Robert was soon promoted to the rank of corporal; then to the rank of detective assigned to the center unit where he investigated residence and business burglaries. During this period he made time to go back to night school at the Metro College where he studied crime investigation. There he met Captain James O'Malley, who was a legend on the Police Force and also one of his instructors at the college. O'Malley was impressed with this young detective and kept him in mind for the next opening he had in his unit. Within a year of meeting Detective Croix, O'Malley interviewed him and was extremely impressed with the officer. Although he had only been on the force for five years and had not yet reached the age of thirty, Croix showed such promise as an up-and-comer that he offered him a position as a detective in the homicide unit. Robert readily accepted. Detective Croix found himself transferred to the homicide division, where he was assigned to the midnight to eight a.m. shift. He was partnered up with one of the older detectives in the unit, whom he got along well with and over the past two years had been involved in numerous homicide investigations with a ninety-two percent clearance rate.

Lately Robert had been spending twelve to eighteen hours a day working on both old and new murder cases he had been assigned to handle, as most of the other members of the squad had their plates full with the two cop murders. At 1:00 a.m. Robert Croix signed out for home. The dispatcher had his apartment telephone number if he was needed. He had the next day off and his intentions were to sleep away his day off. He walked to his vehicle, which was parked on the east lot next to the Headquarter building. Robert approached his vehicle, a red 1938 Chevrolet two-door convertible, which he had purchased only a month before. He loved the soft leather and cloth interior. The engine was a V-8 with a soft purr. He drove out of the H.Q. lot and pulled onto the road. He observed numerous pedestrians still on the street. Most of them ending their night partying and walking home to the safety of their houses or apartments. He couldn't help but smile as he noticed the admiration for his car as he drove past them. He especially enjoyed the attention he and his shiny red Chevrolet received from the females, both young and old, as he passed them. It was good to be alive.

For the past few months, his social life had been pretty much on hold due to his working hours. He guessed that it was best not to get involved to any extent at this time in his life. He lived at the St. Mark Apartments located in a very nice area of the city. It was next to a modern business and shopping area. The residences located around his apartment were those of upper class business people. In his hotel were men and women devoted to the arts, some extremely well-known and successful—others not so well-known. It appeared that all residents came from families with ties to big money.

As Robert pulled into the rear parking garage, he observed his next door neighbor, Diane Car. She waved at him as she exited her car, a black two-door Ford convertible V-8, the same year as Robert's vehicle. Diane was an entertainer who sang with a large band that traveled throughout the states and worked with most of the popular singers of the day. She worked with noted personalities such as Bing Crosby and Frank Sinatra. She had recently cut her own record with the Harry James Band. Robert realized how very attractive she was with her green eyes and long dark hair. She had the stature of a tall woman at five foot seven inches tall and weighed just one hundred fifteen pounds. Diane was wearing a gray pant suit with a white blouse and short-waisted jacket. She looked very much a total woman.

On approaching the entrance to his hotel, Robert noticed Diane was waiting by the door with a beautiful smile directed at him. She had what Robert thought was the whitest teeth he had ever seen and her lips were a soft red color.

"Hi, Diane, you are looking very lovely this early in the morning."

"Why, thank you Robert; it's nice to know someone thinks so—especially after working all evening. I haven't seen you around for a while. Is that police work keeping you busy day and night?"

"Why, yes, it has as a matter of fact, but not so much that it stopped me hearing your new recording on the radio! It was wonderful; you truly have a gifted voice. I enjoy listening to you. In fact I have tickets to watch your performance at the Play-Mor Club next month."

"Wow, Robert; I am impressed. You know how to flatter a woman."

"Well, Diane, I'll take it just a little further; I have ordered a copy of your new recording."

"I am now totally impressed, Robert. I would have given you a copy if I had known you wanted one. In fact I will bring you a copy of it later on today if you are home?"

"Diane, I will make sure to be there."

Robert and Diane both climbed the stairs together to their apartments and said goodbye to each other.

Robert entered his apartment, removed his suit coat, tie and shoes; he immediately turned on his radio and put the dial on the station that played the new hit parade musical numbers. He then dropped into his easy chair and picked up the newspaper and started reading. After a few minutes he found himself getting very sleepy and thought to himself perhaps he would just doze for awhile as he had nothing else planned.

After a refreshing hour's rest, Robert got out of his chair, went to his bedroom, and undressed. He was getting ready to step into his shower when he heard a knock on his apartment door. Who in the hell could that be at this time of the morning as he was not expecting any visitors. Cussing under his breath as he put on a robe and walked to the door, a little irritated, Robert opened the door and stated in a harsh voice, "What do you want?" before he realized that it was his lovely neighbor Diane Car.

"Oh, Robert I am sorry; I thought you would still be up and maybe go with me to get something to eat! I wasn't in the mood for cooking or eating alone."

Diane was wearing a smart looking flowered dress of yellow and white; it accented her beautiful legs and figure.

"I think I would like that very much, Diane; but I need to shower and put on fresh clothes. I won't be more than half an hour."

"That will be fine, Robert. If you don't mind I will wait here in your living room and listen to your radio while you clean up?"

"Great, that will be great," stated Robert. He then left Diane waiting in his front room while he walked back to his bedroom to shower. Robert stepped into his shower, turned on the water, and felt the warmth of the water start to relax his tired muscles. He adjusted the shower to a stronger flow of water and turned his back to it. The gentle beating of water on his shoulders slowed ambitions of a speedy shower. It was pure pleasure and had a recharging effect on his body and mind. In fact, it was exhilarating. Robert started soaping up his body and humming a song when he noticed through the opening in his shower curtains that the door to the bathroom had opened slightly. He watched Diane slip into the small room. The steam from his shower flowed out of the open door giving him a slight chill. Robert watched, although he pretended not to, as Diane dropped her dress and stepped out of it, she then unfastened her bra to reveal a pair of perfectly shaped breasts: firm, pert, pink nipples, slightly upturned. She then placed her thumbs into adjacent sides of the elastic waistband of her panties. She paused before removing her underwear and smiled sweetly at Robert, who by now was aroused.

"You're staring, Robert," she said as she noticed his glances and erection. Her voice was playful and full of promise, as though he was a bad boy peeking through the shower curtains at her.

Diane then dropped her panties to her bare ankles, revealing a soft bush of light brown pubic hair. She pulled open the shower curtain and asked Robert if it was okay to enter his shower. As she stepped into the warm shower she innocently giggled. "Now that you have seen me, Robert; let me see what you've got. She playfully kicked off her panties and entered his shower. The two embraced, then kissed long and hard and satisfied each other's desire there and then as the warm shower water gently added to the erotic tension.

Chapter Twenty-two

Bonacursso and Ryan spent the night and early morning searching for Phil Simone and Vic Gargotta. Both detectives returned to their office in the Headquarters Building. While seated in the homicide squad room writing their reports for the past shift, Bonacursso received a telephone call from an informant.

"You still looking for Phil Simone?" asked the informant in Italian.

"Yes, I am; do you know where I can find him?" Bonacursso responded in Italian.

"How much you pay for that information?"

"Look, motherfucker, don't play games with me. I recognize your fucking voice and I know who you are. I'll make your life miserable if you don't spit out your information. And, asshole, it better not be a lie."

"Shit, Phil; I am just trying to get ahead here; you don't need to threaten me. I could get killed just for talking to you."

"Tell me what you got or I'll be paying your ass a visit, and I know you won't like that!"

"You got to give me something, Phil."

"OK, if your information turns out good I will owe you a favor—nothing more."

"I guess that will have to do for now. So here it is, my friend; I heard from a good source."

"Stop right there, pal; I want to know who you heard the information from before you start telling me your tale."

"Alright, Phil; it was Anthony Gizzo."

"Tell me your story!"

"Gizzo told me that he and Simone, along with Vic Gargotta, had been fucking around at a nigger club on Fifteenth Street on New Year's Eve. Simone was in a card game with those nigger gangsters and got himself killed over money."

"You're sure it was Anthony Gizzo?" asked the detective.

"I wouldn't tell you that if it wasn't true."

"OK, pal; if this information turns out to be good, I'll owe you one." Bonacursso hung up and turned to his partner. "Joe, do we still have Gizzo in custody?"

Joe Ryan replied that they did.

Bonacursso had Anthony Gizzo brought from the jail to the detective's holding cell where he was interrogated by Bonacursso and Ryan. Gizzo was reluctant to talk or give any information to the officers, especially against his friends, now that he had sobered up. Ryan kept questioning the gangster while Bonacursso sat on a chair next to Gizzo. All of a sudden Bonacursso jumped up from his chair and hit the gangster in the face with his fist, breaking Gizzo's nose. Blood sprayed from his nose all over Detective Ryan, who was standing next to him. Bonacursso started to hit him again. The whimpering gangster decided that it would be in his best interest to cooperate and began answering their questions.

"Gizzo, we want to know about the night Simone was killed. We already know what happened and who was involved. I will tell you now if we don't get the truth, I will give your dago ass a beating like you never had before. Then we will book you for attempting to escape. Do you understand?" intoned Bonacursso in a menacing voice.

Ryan started the questioning and asked, "In what bar was Simone killed?"

"One on Fifteenth Street."

"Where on Fifteenth Street, shithead?"

"At that fucking nigger joint owned by Jonas Carter. I don't know the name of the place."

"Was Jonas Carter there when Simone was killed?"

"Yes, Carter was there along with his gang."

"How was Simone killed?"

"He was shot by one of those niggers he had been playing cards with."

"Why was he shot?"

"Listen, Ryan; I don't know for sure why he was shot. I think he thought they were cheating him and he was drunk enough to start some shit with one of them and got himself shot and killed."

"What happened to Simone's body?"

"I don't know; it was left in Carter's hands to dispose of the body. We left; we didn't want any more trouble, and you know every one of those niggers had guns. You cops won't let anyone know I told you, will you?"

"Not at all," smiled Bonacursso.

Bonacursso and Ryan were waiting in O'Malley's office when the Captain arrived for work. They gave him the information they had learned from the informant and Gizzo.

"Has anyone talked to Jonas Carter yet?" O'Malley wanted to know.

"No, we just got the information about an hour ago, and we haven't done anything in regard to Mr. Carter," replied Bonacursso.

"Good, in fact, great. You two just might have solved a homicide. Sergeant Walker and I will pay Carter a visit today and follow up on this. I want you two to write up your reports; then go home and get some sleep."

At 11:00 a.m., O'Malley and Walker drove to Jonas Carter's saloon. They entered the establishment and walked to the bar area. A trio of musicians was playing jazz favorites on a small stage. The bar was pretty full of customers for being so early. The two detectives listened a few moments to the music. No one seemed to take notice of the two officers even though the bar patrons were mostly black.

There were some whites scattered throughout the saloon. Shortly the bartender noticed the two men standing at the bar and walked over to them. He asked what they were drinking. O'Malley ordered two black coffees. When the barman returned with their coffee, he asked if either one of the men wanted anything else. O'Malley told the man that he wanted to talk with Jonas Carter. The bartender informed him that he was in his back office and he would get Carter for them. The bartender then disappeared to the back area of the saloon. In a few moments, both the bartender and Jonas appeared.

"O'Malley and Walker; it's kind of early for you two to be in a bar. Is police work that slow?" asked Carter.

"No, we are here to talk to you about an incident that occurred in this bar around New Year's. Do you want to talk here or in your office?"

"Oh, I guess it's best to talk in my office, O'Malley. Follow me." The detectives followed Carter to his office where they all three had a seat.

"Well, O'Malley, did my information turn out to be correct?"

"Yes, it did; but I have learned since our meeting that you lied to me!"

"What do you mean I lied to you?"

"When I asked if you knew anything about Phil Simone and Vic Gargotta, you told me that you knew nothing about them. But I discovered that wasn't true; you know plenty! You held back on me, but asked me to help you with certain favors to stop political pressure from city politicians and certain thugs wanting to take over your territories. Now, Jonas, do you have more to tell me?"

"Ah, look Captain, Gargotta scares me more than those political assholes do. I can't be seen telling a story about them. If I did I would end up dead."

"I won't bullshit you, Jonas, and tell you I can protect you. But I will tell you if you don't talk, I will promise you that I will fuck you over your silence concerning this matter."

"Look, O'Malley, if there is any way that whatever I tell you is kept from getting me involved or pointing to me I might help you. Can you keep my name out of this?"

"We can work that out as long as you didn't kill anyone I'm interested in."

"OK, O'Malley, I trust you; you never fucked me over before. Does that also go for your partner here about not saying anything to anyone about what I tell you?"

"My work is the same as Sergeant Walker's; we both keep our promises. Does that answer your question?"

"Alright. On New Year's Eve night, Phil Simone, Vic Gargotta, and Anthony Gizzo came into my bar together. All three of them had been drinking before coming in here. It was apparent that Simone was drunker than the others, and I think he was looking for trouble. He got involved in a high-end card game going on with some big-time gangsters. He lost a lot of money and got angry over it. He pulled a gun, I think to rob the other players. One of the players pulled his own gun and shot Simone dead."

"What did Simone's two friends do?"

"Gargotta and the other man pulled out their guns to control the situation and ordered me to dispose of Simone's body and keep my mouth shut. They then left and the boys hauled Simone's ass to the dump site along the river. I swear, O'Malley, that's all I know."

As O'Malley listened to Carter, he knew that the man was telling the truth and that Carter had just put his life in their hands. O'Malley stated to Carter that he believed him and would not mention his involvement. He had other sources he could use if he ever needed to. The detectives then left the tavern and returned to headquarters in order to make some plans for the next step in their investigation—locating Gargotta.

Chapter Twenty-three

Captain James Patrick O'Bryan had been enjoying a drink with some friends at one of his favorite bars which reflected his Irish heritage. The bar was known as Ryan O'Tool's Lounge. Many police officers spent many hours of the day and night drinking at this lounge. Most of the time, what they drank was on the house. What most of them didn't know was that the lounge was owned by the North End Mob and fronted by Ryan O'Tool. Even if the police personnel had known, it probably would have made no difference. Most of them owed their souls to the mob.

After a few drinks, O'Bryan told his pals that he was tired and was going home to get a good night's sleep. He checked his watch and saw that it was 8:00 p.m. The police captain glanced at the wall calendar on the tavern wall and saw that the date was Monday, March 7, 1940. "It's been one of those long days, and I am really looking forward to my bed," he had informed his friends as he left the lounge.

O'Bryan walked to his apartment, which was only two blocks from the tavern. As he walked, his mind was bothered again about the tip he had given to that Morgan guy concerning the killer Kaymark. Not that he had any remorse—but that he should have held out for more money. After all, it could come back on him if something happened as a result of giving out that information.

Perhaps he could contact Morgan in the morning and try to put the squeeze on him for a little more money.

The captain was now entering the entryway of his apartment building. It had been raining slightly as he walked home, and he was now starting to get wet. He slowly climbed the rug-covered steps to his apartment which was located on the second floor. He had been living at this same location for the last ten years.

His apartment, according to every female he had ever brought there, was very tastefully decorated. He tried to change the decor every six months just to impress the women that he brought home. Although he lived by himself and preferred it that way, he did enjoy the company of a woman every now and then.

O'Bryan put his key in the door lock, pushed the door open, and entered the apartment. As soon as he entered, he had a feeling that something was wrong. He thought that he had left a lamp on in his front room as this was his normal habit. He thought that maybe the light bulb had burned out. "Shit," he stated out loud, "always something wrong." He then reached for the wall light switch to turn on the overhead light when he noticed a shadow moving to his right. Then he felt an arm going around his neck and pulling his head back in a violent arch. A stinging pain seared his brain as an ice pick was forced into his ear and into his brain. O'Bryan thought he had screamed as he fell backward to the floor, but no noise uttered from his throat. His body started to spasm and his legs kicked; his bladder turned loose and his trousers were wet with urine that ran onto the rug.

The Police Captain could still hear, although he was in severe pain and unable to move. He heard the footfalls of his assailant as he walked to the apartment door and closed it. He felt the offender standing over him, then heard the click of a knife being opened. The offender then knelt down beside the dying captain and rolled him over onto his back. He again pulled his head back by the hair. This time he inserted the knife into his throat, cutting it from ear to ear. All the while he told the captain, "Don Torrio sends his regards, you greedy cocksucker."

The killer then searched the apartment and found three thousand dollars in a dresser in the bedroom. He placed the money in his pocket and then checked the rest of the apartment for money. He was in no hurry now that he had dispatched his target to another world—probably hell if you believed in that crap. He didn't.

The killer returned to the body of Captain O'Bryan and felt for any sign of life. He was then satisfied that the captain was dead. He then checked the captain's pockets and found another five hundred dollars. He smiled and stated to the corpse, "Crime really didn't pay well for you." Vic Gargotta then left the apartment and disappeared into the night.

Chapter Twenty-four

On March 5, 1940, three men entered a high-end jewelry store at Ninth Street and McGee. All three had rushed into the store. One of them locked the front door and then pulled a sawed-off shotgun from under the coat he was wearing. The other two men had pulled revolvers from their waistbands and accosted the customers and employees who were in the store. They announced that it was a holdup and that they wanted everyone to get down on their knees and keep their mouth shut or they would be killed. Everyone complied.

The one giving the orders was around six feet tall. He had a fleshy, prominent nose, dark hair, thick mustache and mean-looking black eyes. His teeth were broken in front and stained brown—probably from tobacco. He had powerful looking arms and walked with the quiet fluidity of a cat. According to all the witnesses, he appeared to be of Italian descent. The other two men were not so tall, but also dark skinned. One of these two men walked with a slight limp. The other robber had poor posture and slumped. He also had graying hair. All three of the robbers spoke with broken English. None of the men had even attempted to hide their faces. All three of them wore full-length coats and sported dark colored wide-brimmed hats.

The leader of the robbers wanted to know who was the manager. When the manager spoke up and identified himself, he was grabbed by the leader and struck across the face with the back of the bandit's hand. His face and lips immediately swelled. The manager was then told, "Open your safe or I'll fucking kill you." The leader of the three then pointed to the gray-haired bandit and stated, "Gather up all the jewelry in the display cases, and put everything in a bag." The gray-haired robber did just that.

The leader, with the manager in tow, then walked to a back room of the store where the safe was located. The manager was again ordered to open the safe. The manager hesitated and received a lacerating blow to his head from a revolver held by the bandit. The leader then cocked the revolver hammer back and held it to the manager's face, stating, "OK, motherfucker, either open the safe or your brains will be all over it." The manager opened the safe while his head bled profusely.

"Fill this bag with all the jewels and cash in that safe." The manager complied at once.

One of the robbers yelled to the leader, "What is that foul smell?"

"Nothing," replied the leader, "this fucking guy just shit his pants." The manager was brought to the front of the store where he was told to lay down.

The three robbers left the store with twenty thousand dollars worth of jewelry and eight thousand dollars in cash. They ran down the street and entered a blue Ford four-door and sped away. Vic Gargotta, the leader, who was riding in the front passenger seat of the speeding car, noticed a police car pull in behind them. The gray-haired robber also noticed the police unit and panicked. He shot at the police and missed.

The police officers returned gunfire. Gargotta and the gray-haired bandit had their driver slow the automobile while they exited and exchanged shots with the police officers. The gray-haired gangster fell to the street after being fatally shot in the chest and head. The other robber made good his escape, but not before the two officers both recognized him as Vic Gargotta. The policemen also noticed that the getaway vehicle was standing in the middle of the road about a hundred yards down the street. As they approached the automobile, they discovered that the driver was slumped over the steering wheel with a hole in his head and his face splattered on the inside window.

Detectives Bonacursso and Ryan responded to the scene of the shootings as they were already in the area looking for Gargotta and Simone. They started their investigation by looking over the dead mobsters and then examining the mobster's vehicle. Inside the car they found a bag full of jewelry and a sack of money. It appeared that the bad men had made no profit in their robbery. The detectives were then informed that a jewelry store manager was reporting to other detectives that he had been robbed by three guys who made their getaway in a Ford fitting the description of the vehicle they had at the scene of the shootings. The uniformed policemen who exchanged shots with the gangsters told the detectives they recognized the one that escaped on foot as Vic Gargotta.

Detective Ryan put out a pickup order for robbery and assault on Vic Gargotta. Then he notified Captain O'Malley, who first responded to the jewelry store and contacted the officers working that case. He then drove to the scene of the shooting and contacted his two detectives there.

March 6, 1940: 0500 hours

An unmarked United States Army sedan pulled into the headquarters building basement garage and parked in an area marked for prisoner loading and unloading. Three men exited the vehicle and walked to the jail elevator, pressed the up button, and waited. All three of the men were attired in civilian suits, not military uniforms. The elevator arrived and opened to a uniformed policeman who was operating it. He looked at the three men and questioned their reason for being there. The men showed their identifications and showed the police officer their orders to take into military custody Kaymark and transport him to Fort Leavenworth, Kansas. The three men were then allowed to enter the elevator and were taken to the city jail. They then presented their identifications and military orders to take custody of Mr. Kaymark upon demand by the desk sergeant.

The desk sergeant examined their paperwork and warrant. He then told the men that they would have to wait about ten minutes while the jail personnel processed the prisoner out of jail custody and into military custody. Kaymark was soon turned over to the three men. One of the military personnel placed handcuffs on the prisoner. Then all four of the men returned to the military vehicle.

"Where you guys taking me?" asked Kaymark.

"Well, pal; you're going straight to Leavenworth for processing. Then you will be turned over to the Intelligence Unit of the Army. So, Mr. Kaymark, sit back and enjoy the ride; it will take about two hours," one of the three told him.

Vic Gargotta was in the company of another man whom he didn't know. But he was told by Don Zino Torrio to do exactly what this man instructed him to do and to do it right. At a location just outside of the Leavenworth Highway, Gargotta was ordered to park the vehicle they had been riding in.

Gargotta was instructed to wait for an O.D. colored unmarked military sedan which would contain four men. "Three of these men are investigators for the military; the fourth is a traitor to his country. It is not important that you know any of their names, only that we are going to kill all of them and set their car on fire. I will be in the bushes on the left side of the street and will shoot the driver. That should bring the car to a stop or cause it to crash. You will then shoot the other three men. Make sure they are all dead. I will then set the car on fire. We will leave in this vehicle and return to the city. Do you understand my instructions, Gargotta?" asked his companion.

"Yes, I understand."

"Do you have any questions?"

"No," replied Gargotta.

"It is my understanding that you will be paid by Mr. Torrio for your services."

"Yes, that is true," replied Gargotta.

The two men exited the vehicle without a comment and walked to the rear of their car. They opened the trunk where they removed two weapons, a 303 Springfield rifle with scope and a Thompson 80-round type sub-machine gun. Gargotta checked the machine gun's action. He felt satisfied with the feel as he had used this type of weapon before and was very proficient with it. The other man worked the action on the rifle, checked his ammunition, and put the rifle on safety. Both men then took up their positions for the ambush.

It was approximately 6:50 a.m. The morning was slightly foggy with a light rain starting to fall. The man with the rifle observed the military sedan traveling on the two-lane road at approximately forty-five miles per hour. It was the only vehicle on this road and the first one that they had seen since their arrival. As the vehicle approached the ambush killing zone, the man with the rifle could see that this was indeed his target vehicle. He took aim and fired the rifle, hitting the driver in the head. The car ran off the road into a water ditch and stopped. There was panic in the automobile as Gargotta approached with his machine gun and opened up on the helpless men. He emptied the weapon's fire power into the vehicle and bodies of the men until he ran out of bullets.

The man with the rifle returned to the trunk of their vehicle and placed the rifle inside, removed a five gallon can of gas, returned to the military automobile, splashed the gasoline over the interior of the car and over the bodies of the three military men, and soaked the dead body of Kaymark thoroughly. He then struck a match and set the car aflame. Gargotta ran to the trunk of their vehicle and placed the machine gun inside while the other man put the gas can inside. Both men watched as the military vehicle burned. Gargotta was surprised that there was no other traffic on the road. Then they drove back to the city.

Chapter Twenty-five

Around noon, the Desk Sergeant at the City Jail became concerned that he had not seen or heard from his Commanding Officer in the last three days. The Commanding Officer had not scheduled any days off and had no vacation time on the books. The Desk Sergeant called his Captain's apartment several times without success. Furthermore, the Desk Sergeant had received information just a few moments ago from the County Sheriff's Office that one of Kansas City's former inmates by the name of Kaymark, along with his escort of military policemen, had been ambushed near the Kansas state line in Platte County, Missouri. All four men had been killed. According to the Sheriff's Office, the military sedan that the four men were traveling in had been set on fire. The occupants of the vehicle had been burned to a crisp. The Sheriff's Office had learned the names of the military personnel from the United States Army Military Police at Fort Leavenworth, Kansas. These military personnel were escorting Mr. Kaymark to their base. The Sheriff stated that he was giving Kansas City Police Department a heads up on what had occurred since the Army wanted it kept out of the newspapers. The Sheriff's Office was turning the case over to the military.

The Desk Sergeant called the Homicide Unit and contacted Captain James O'Malley to advise him of the incident reported to him by the Platte County Sheriff's Department. The Sergeant then apologized to O'Malley for not reporting it up through his Commanding Officer. He told O'Malley that he had not been able to contact his Commanding Officer for several days and felt that the information could not wait since it involved one of their former inmates.

The Desk Sergeant then had a police unit dispatched to his Captain's apartment to ascertain if the Commander was all right and to have the Captain call him as soon as possible.

After the conversation with the Desk Sergeant, O'Malley made a phone call to the Platte County Sheriff's office and talked to the Detective who had handled the case and was at the scene of the military vehicle. He informed O'Malley what he had found at the scene. He also told O'Malley two other things. First, he believed that the military vehicle and its occupants were ambushed at the location where they found the vehicle still smoking from the fire. He further noticed that the vehicle had been riddled with bullet holes—at least twenty. Second, the case had been completely taken over by the Army and Federal Bureau of Investigation. We were told in no uncertain terms to keep out of their way and not to give the press any information concerning this incident. "When I asked why they didn't want our help I was told, in no uncertain terms, to forget about the case, that my Department wasn't qualified. Can you believe that shit? Oh well, that's four less homicides we need to worry about. Anything else you need from me, Captain?"

"No, you have been a big help, and thanks a lot for the information, Detective."

O'Malley then called the Chief of Detectives, John Miller, and related the information he had so far received on the incident. Miller then notified his boss, the Chief of Police.

O'Malley had no sooner hung up his phone when the Police Dispatcher called him and stated that a District car was requesting a Homicide Unit at the apartment of Captain O'Bryan. "It appears that he was the victim of a robbery gone bad," stated the Dispatcher. O'Malley assigned Detectives Ryan and Bonacursso to respond to the scene and start the investigation into the homicide. O'Malley then re-dialed the Chief of Detectives and made contact with his boss, John Miller. He gave Miller what information he had concerning Captain O'Bryan.

O'Malley leaned back in his chair and sipped a cup of lukewarm coffee. He was running through the events of the last few hours and wondered if there could be any connection between Captain O'Bryan's death and the ambush of Kaymark. He had no evidence that put the two events together other than coincidence, and he didn't believe in coincidence. O'Malley called his Operations Sergeant, John Walker, to his office to discus his thoughts.

"Shit, Jim, another police homicide; that's going to look great in the papers!"

"My thought exactly! John, here is what I want you to do. Respond to Captain O'Bryan's apartment and make sure nothing is overlooked. Then, if time allows, contact Colonel Small. He might shed more light on the Kaymark incident."

"You got it, Boss." Walker grabbed his suit coat and headed out the door.

Chapter Twenty-six

Peter Morgan and Vic Gargotta returned to Kansas City after the ambush of the Military Police and Kaymark. Morgan instructed his companion to drive him to the Union Station. Upon arrival, Morgan again gave Gargotta orders to get rid of the weapons and the car, but not in Kansas City. He was to dump the weapons in the Missouri River and drop the automobile in an area isolated from the normal flow of traffic on the Kansas side.

Morgan then walked into the Union Station. He continued to the Western Union counter where he made out a cryptic telegram and sent it to a Professor Michaels at Harvard College. He paid for the telegram and exited to the taxi area and had the driver of the cab drop him off at his hotel. When in his room, he made a few phone calls and set up a meeting with some of his associates and the old don Torrio.

Morgan rented a 1938 Desoto four-door sedan from a rental agency located next to his hotel. He then drove to the city airport. Morgan waited in the airport terminal for several hours while waiting for a flight to arrive from Boston, Massachusetts. Several cups of coffee later, Morgan heard the aircraft arrival being announced. It would unload at gate number five. He found an area to stand in next to the unloading gate. Soon Morgan saw and greeted three men who all knew each other well. Morgan walked with the men to pick up their luggage and then escorted them to his rented vehicle. He drove to his hotel where they had a meal and then all retired to his suite.

These four men all had two things in common—they were all Intelligence Officers in the German Army SS Group and they were all very good at sabotage and were stone cold killers. The three new arrivals spoke and understood the English language and they were absolute fanatics concerning their assignments. All answered to Morgan. The three new arrivals had been secretly brought into the American east coast by submarine. They disembarked in Maine, where they stayed at a safe house until they received orders to report to Kansas City, Missouri, and meet up with Morgan.

Morgan poured highballs for his guests, and then stated in German, "You men know why you are here. We are going to work with the criminal element of this city as well as a few well-placed politicians. None of them will know our true mission here. These criminals will be led to believe that we are criminals out of the Boston area who have some inside information concerning hi-jacking and train burglaries. We will share the burglaries and other crimes of profit with them on a 50/50 cut. They will be required to supply us with additional man power and they will do all the fencing of materials stolen, no matter what. We will allow them to make some money from our thought-out offenses. What you men and myself will be doing is distracting the law enforcement organizations into thinking it's just gangsters hi-jacking merchandise. I will be contacted by infiltrated military sources when a secret project of the United States is ready for shipment. They will give me the location and time when it will pass through here in Kansas City. We will steal it and forward it to our people. All the time the Police will blame it on the city's gangsters—never realizing that the German intelligence was behind the thefts."

Morgan refilled his guests' glasses and made a salute to their future and that of their homeland. "Tonight, gentlemen, we will meet with some of this criminal element and plan a few hi-jackings that will make some money for these people. Freight will be the type of hi-jacking I will plan for them. You all speak English well.

Never use our language; always speak in English. Never talk to these criminals about yourselves. I want you to always carry a firearm and use it if you need to!"

Morgan then looked at his watch and indicated they were to drive over to the residence of a Mr. Torrio, the head of the Kansas City Criminal Cartel, and a few of his men.

After meeting with the old don Torrio, Morgan felt certain that the meeting was very productive. Morgan produced several freight line manifests and their listed cargo. The mobsters were delirious with greed. The hi-jackings would start with the group breaking into train boxcars that had been secretly placed on different rail tracks and guarded by railroad police in the central industrial part of the city.

The German spies would start doing a little effective sabotage in addition to the other crimes.

Chapter Twenty-seven

Detectives Ryan and Bonacursso were back at the Homicide Unit preparing to write their investigation reports around 10:00 p.m. Sergeant Walker returned to the Unit shortly and reported all the information he had gleaned through his investigation. Walker, upon arrival at the apartment of Captain O'Bryan and after conferring with Ryan and Bonacursso, discovered that the assailant of O'Bryan had laid in wait inside the apartment and murdered the Captain with what appeared to be an ice pick. The ice pick had entered his right ear and continued into his brain, and his throat had been cut from ear to ear. The way O'Bryan was murdered looked more like a mob hit. It was cold, quick, and very professional. No money had been found on the corpse or in his apartment.

Sergeant Walker had found that the Captain lived way beyond his income as a Police Captain. Furthermore, they found a couple of different bank books hidden in his files in the office at the apartment. These bank books indicated he had accumulated over one hundred thousand dollars from 1933 to 1940. The furnishings in his apartment were very expensive. His closet revealed thirty different suits easily costing three hundred dollars each. He also owned silk shirts which had been custom-made and very expensive jewelry. His shoes were custom-made from a local shoe maker.

Sergeant Walker had checked out the banks O'Bryan had money in and discovered that he had a safety deposit box. The box held several thousand dollars along with numerous deeds of purchase throughout the metro area and into Kansas. Walker also found a journal in O'Bryan's own handwriting in the box. This journal listed many of his connections to criminals throughout the area. It appeared that the Captain had some heavy connections to the underworld. In this journal, O'Bryan had written about many unsolved crimes that he had arranged and became physically involved in. These included burglaries, murders, and other hanging crimes. When Sergeant Walker had finished reading the journal he had the names of at least fifty police officers who were either on the take or involved in committing the crimes. It seemed that Captain O'Bryan was getting kickbacks from almost every police officer mentioned in this book.

"It's just fucking unreal and hard to believe that we have that many police officers who have sold their souls!" grunted Walker.

"Shit, John, look how many the new Chief has fired in this last year—almost 40 per cent of the Force due to corruption. It appears that when Internal Affairs gets hold of this list, there will be a lot more fired or prosecuted. By the way, I have already had O'Bryan's office locked and sealed. John, you and I will search it and interview his staff tomorrow."

"Also, John, I am going to wake up the Chief and our boss and feed them all of the information we have before I go home—if I even get to go home today!"

"Hell, James, it might be easier if I came with you."

"Good, I always love catching hell for waking up the brass and giving them bad news."

After telephoning the two superior officers, they all agreed to meet at Detective Chief Miller's home in one hour.

Chapter Twenty-eight

On the drive over to the Chief's home, O'Malley asked Walker if he had made contact with Colonel Small in regards to the incident with Kaymark.

"No, Jim; I was not able to make contact with the Colonel today. I just had too much on my plate. I am surprised that you haven't been contacted by him! Maybe he skipped over Homicide and went right to the Chief's Office."

"Could be, as he may also have too much on his plate. But you can bet he will. I suspect he is way too good of an investigator not to realize that there had been a leak concerning the time that Kaymark was being released from our custody to the Army."

"Hell, Jim, the only one who knew when Kaymark was to be moved was the Chief himself or maybe the Chief of Detectives."

The two Detectives arrived at the Chief's home at 4:30 a.m. The Police Chief and his Chief of Detectives, John Miller, were both enjoying a fresh cup of coffee that the Police Chief's wife had made for them. O'Malley and Walker were met at the door by the Chief's wife, Helen. Helen led both Detectives into the kitchen where the Chief stood and shook hands with the two newcomers. The Detective Chief also shook their hands. Helen poured all of them a hot cup of coffee. She then left the kitchen so that the four officers could feel free to talk.

"Okay, James, what is going on?" asked the Chief.

"First, Chief, Captain O'Bryan was found murdered in his apartment. He had been stabbed in the head with what we believe to be an ice pick. His throat was cut from eat to ear."

"What was it, a home robbery gone bad?" questioned the Chief.

"No, sir; it is our opinion that Captain O'Bryan himself was the target."

"You mean to tell me the Captain was assassinated?" asked the Chief.

"It appears that way, and furthermore, there was a message in the way he was murdered."

"O'Malley, how in the hell did you come to this conclusion?"

"In our reconstruction of the crime scene we found no forced entry into the apartment. It appears that O'Bryan was attacked as soon as he walked into his apartment. The lights were not turned on. Of course, the Medical Examiner thinks he had been dead for several hours. Although we found no cash on the person of O'Bryan and none laying around the apartment, we have learned from some of his friends that he always carried a large amount of cash. The first detectives to respond to the scene found that the Captain still had his service revolver holstered on his belt on the right side of his body. Sergeant Walker here also responded to the death scene shortly after the two lead detectives, Ryan and Bonacursso, and took charge of the investigation and crime scene."

"By the way, both of the Detectives are top-notch investigators," interjected Sergeant Walker.

"Sergeant Walker can fill you in with what he found at the apartment," stated O'Malley.

"First, sir, I discovered bank books at Captain O'Bryan's apartment."

"Bank books, you mean more than one?" questioned the Chief.

"Yes, sir, we found several of O'Bryan's bank accounts where he had socked large sums of money throughout the years. I then checked the banks that held the accounts. I discovered that he had stored away more money than he and all of us would make in thirty years."

"Did his apartment show a style of living beyond his means as a Police Captain?" asked John Miller.

"Yes, he lived way beyond his means as a policeman."

"O'Malley, from what I am hearing it seems that O'Bryan was a dirty cop!" stated the Chief as he shook his head and became quiet.

"Chief, you haven't heard anything yet! While checking one of his accounts at the First National Bank of Kansas City, I discovered that he had a safety deposit box. That safety deposit box contained thousands of dollars in cash along with real estate holdings and a large journal written in O'Bryan's penmanship. The journal contained crimes that he had either masterminded or committed himself over the years and who he did them with. It appears he had close ties to organized crime. He listed numerous officers of our department and those of other agencies on the take."

"O'Malley, do you know how many officers of our department are dirty according to the journal?!"

"Approximately fifty that are still in the department."

"Son of a bitch; Miller, how in the fuck did we miss these dirty cops over the past year?"

"Shit, Chief; that's an easy one. It was called home rule, where gangsters and politicians ran the department with a free hand and the city enjoyed being the center of vice and crime. Hell, boss, we have only been under state control for the last fifteen months. Since going under state control, we have fired or prosecuted forty per cent of the department. We just haven't learned who all have been involved in corruption until now."

"When I left the FBI to run this department, I knew it had problems. But never did I think it was this corrupt! Goddamn it, will this department ever in the next fifty years live this shit down? Here it is again, police corruption. I guess nothing can be done about the past, just improve the department as we move along."

"Chief," intoned O'Malley, "we might have another problem, the Kaymark case."

"What are you talking about; wasn't that case turned over to the Army?"

"It was, Chief, but Kaymark along with his Army escort apparently was ambushed in Platte County. All four men were murdered by assailants unknown to us at this time. This ambush occurred approximately an hour or two after they left the Headquarters Building."

Sergeant Walker then reported the entire incident as it was related to him.

"What has the Army had to say about the incident?" asked the Chief.

O'Malley blushed slightly and stated, "We haven't heard from the Army as yet. I am going to contact Colonel Small sometime this morning or whenever I can reach him."

"O'Malley, where is the O'Bryan journal now?"

"It's in my office safe, Chief."

"O'Malley, is it safe there?" asked Chief of Detectives John Miller.

"Yes, sir; in the morning Sergeant Walker will have a copy made for you and Chief Miller."

"Has the press gotten wind of these events yet?"

"No, sir; they haven't gotten any information from us nor have they asked."

"My next question to you three; should I go ahead and turn this over to Internal Affairs or hold it for now?"

"Chief, I think we should wait until our investigation is further along. At this point, we don't know who to trust with our information. Also, when we get ready to release the information, let's turn it over to your old Department of Justice, the FBI."

The Chief then asked O'Malley how the investigation was going on the two murdered police officers.

"We are still working on it with no real development. It seems as though no one wants to talk to us about it. However, we have a few ideas we are following up on."

"Fuck! Fuck!" stated Chief of Detectives Miller. "Can't the Department ever get a break? O'Malley, solve this thing and do it goddamned quick."

Helen stuck her head back in the kitchen and asked her husband how many would be staying for breakfast. He informed her that there would be four.

O'Malley and Walker left the home of the Chief after breakfast and drove back to their office. Shortly after the Commander and his Operations Sergeant arrived, they met with Detective Robert Croix who was just signing in for work. Croix was assigned to get the O'Bryan journal copied in secret and ready for Captain O'Malley at the end of Croix' shift. He was also informed to use a trustworthy typist.

O'Malley telephoned the Military Base at Fort Leavenworth, Kansas, and requested that Colonel Small telephone him after 6:00 p.m.

For the next hour O'Malley and Walker searched Captain O'Bryan's office. While checking old teletypes, Sergeant Walker discovered the communication from Chief of Detectives Miller ordering the release of Kaymark to the Army.

"Look at this, Jim. It's where O'Bryan initialed the order to release."

"Guess that tells us who leaked the information on Kaymark."

"It's 9:30 a.m. Let's you and I go get a few hours sleep. Meet in the office at 6:00 p.m.," ordered O'Malley.

Detective Croix completed his assignment of copying the journal given to him by O'Malley. He sat in the squad room reading the copies for any typing errors. As he read over O'Bryan's journal, he was spellbound with who he saw listed as dirty cops. Some of the names he noticed were Patrol Commanders. According to this account of O'Bryan's, many had ties with the north end mob and corrupt politicians of the past and present. Thank God no detectives of his unit were listed.

Chapter Twenty-nine

O'Malley entered his office around 0530 hours and found Detective Robert Croix waiting for him with the journal and six typed copies of it.

"Captain, here is the journal you wanted copies of in secret. No one, other than the typist and myself, know about it and what it contains. I assure you that the typist is one of the most trustworthy in the department and has been privy to many secret memos and other events."

"Good, Robert; I appreciate the time and work you put into getting it finished by this morning. One copy goes to the Police Chief, one copy to the Chief of Detectives John Miller, and one for the Internal Affairs Unit. The journal and the rest of the copies I will put in the office safe after I mark all as secret and confidential. I will require you to sign your name to all copies and I will sign my name under your signature."

Sergeant John Walker entered the office with a large cup of coffee and a thermos.

"Bringing your own coffee to work, Sergeant?" asked O'Malley with a grin on his face.

"You bet, Boss; My wife got up and made me an outstanding breakfast and made a thermos of wonderful black coffee because I tell her how nasty the coffee is here at the office—especially the way you make it."

"Oh, fuck you, John," laughed O'Malley.

"Tell you what I will do, Jim. I'll share some with you two, but you better get it before the rest of the squad gets here 'cause those fellows will finish the coffee off in a flash."

"No thanks, Sergeant. I am coffeed out," Croix said with a grimace on his face.

"Long night was it now, Detective," asked the Sergeant as he poured O'Malley a cup of coffee from his thermos.

O'Malley, after putting the journal and the copies in his safe, dismissed Detective Croix and sent him home to get some sleep.

"Jim, it's going on twelve weeks now since the murders of the two patrolmen, and we have nothing that we can give the press as yet."

"You're right, John, so let's allow the Chief of Detectives to handle the press boys. He has been bullshitting them for years."

Detectives Bonacursso and Ryan entered the squad office together, grabbed two cups of coffee, and entered O'Malley's office. They were brought up to date on O'Malley and Walker's meeting with the Chief and Detective Chief Miller earlier that morning. O'Malley wanted to know if the officers had been contacted by any informants concerning Gargotta. Both detectives stated they had not, and it appeared that no one wanted to talk about him.

"If we are going to catch the cocksucker, Captain, I think we will have to put a lot more pressure on the mob until it really hurts. Maybe we can get the press to help by keeping Gargotta's mug in the papers every day until he is in custody. We can tell them we will give the press boys a good story after we capture him," stated Ryan.

Bonacursso told his teammates and commander that they knew Gargotta was controlled by none other than Zino Torrio and was considered one of the top torpedoes in the rackets. If they couldn't locate Gargotta within the next twenty-four hours someone needed to have a sit-down talk with Zino.

O'Malley informed all present to start closing down all gambling and brothels controlled by Torrio in the city and to arrest as many of Zino's people as possible. After a couple of days of this type of police heat O'Malley would embarrass Torrio by arresting him on some minor bullshit charge—maybe as a pimp—and having the newspapers print it for all respectable people to read and point their fingers at him. O'Malley would then interrogate the son-of-a-bitch in person.

Chapter Thirty

At 10:00 a.m., O'Malley was contacted by Colonel Small of Army Intelligence by telephone.

"Captain O'Malley, I understand that you have been attempting to contact me."

"Yes, Colonel, that was four days ago."

"Well, you must realize how busy we have been since the ambush on Mr. Kaymark and my men."

"Yes, I can appreciate what must be going on in your investigation of the homicides. Is there anything I can do from my end?"

There was a long pause before the Colonel spoke again. "You know, Captain O'Malley, only three people besides myself on my end knew anything about us picking up Kaymark and the date and time of us taking him into custody. The other was you, your Chief of Detectives, and the Police Chief."

"What are you implying, Colonel?"

"Simple, O'Malley, I think your department leaked the information. I have talked with the FBI agents assigned to this investigation, and they suspect the same thing. Your department doesn't inspire us to place any trust in it. Your police department is widely notorious for corruption from the top to the bottom."

"Look, Colonel; I'm not even going to attempt to defend the department. The past history is what it is—a total disgrace. With that said, I can assure you that my unit and team is beyond that. I fully trust each and every one of my men with my life."

"O.K., O'Malley, I believe you and your sincerity. Let's get together tomorrow and do some talking—a professional exchange of information—just you and me."

"Where?" asked O'Malley.

"I will call you and tell you where."

The Army Colonel then hung up on O'Malley. James O'Malley sat and mentally went over everything he knew about the Kaymark incident. Unless the military had other information that he was not aware of (and they just might), he suspected that the leak did indeed come from someone within the Police Department. He was sure that person was the recently murdered Captain O'Bryan of the Detention Unit. Everything pointed in his direction. O'Malley's mood turned dark, and his eyes reflected his inner thoughts to such an extent that his Operations Sergeant Walker noticed it and asked his boss and friend what was going on.

"We still have a very sick department, John! I think we are going to have to guard ourselves even more than before it became state controlled. I think we are going to have to turn our detectives loose with their own devices to get the information we need to close these two cases."

"Jim, are you talking about the homicides of the two patrolmen and the Kaymark incident?"

"Yes, John; my gut tells me they are related somehow."

Chapter Thirty-one

Colonel Small telephoned O'Malley and agreed to meet with him at the Continental Hotel in Kansas City. The Colonel noticed as he entered the hotel that it was one of the most lavish in modern decor that Kansas City entertained. The lobby rugs were plush, and most of the patrons of the hotel would agree that walking on the carpet was like walking on air. The rug was a dark maroon color and very expensive. The bar area for off-the-street customers was located to the right of the lobby. The floor of the bar shined highly in the reflective lights from the barroom stage lights. The floor was black marble cut in a diamond shape. The bar itself was massive with a wooden oak countertop that was waxed so smooth that glasses or ash trays would float over the bar when pushed toward a waiting customer. In a corner a few feet from the bar was the stage for entertainment. At present, a small group was playing a soft set of jazz notes.

Colonel Small observed O'Malley sitting by himself in a darkened corner of the room. He was nursing an iced drink. As Small approached, O'Malley raised his drink in a salute and smiled. Small returned the greeting, walked toward O'Malley's table, and took a seat. He stopped a passing waitress and ordered a highball, lit up a Camel cigarette from a package he had been holding, and offered one to O'Malley. O'Malley refused with a wave of his hand.

Small then took a deep draw into his lungs and looked around the bar as though looking for something or someone.

Small then looked directly into O'Malley's eyes and stated, "O'Malley, I think you and I can work together."

"As do I," replied O'Malley. "However, only if we don't keep secrets from each other. If we can't do that, then I have other cases to work on."

Colonel Small thought for a few moments and just watched the policeman before he answered. "I trust you, O'Malley, and everything I have discovered about you shows you to be an honest and intelligent law enforcement officer. I will keep no information from you. If it's something that I can't give you, I will say so. But as far as the Kaymark case, I will give you all the information I am allowed."

"That's fair enough, Colonel Small."

"O.K., Jim, may I call you by your first name?"

"Sure," replied O'Malley.

"Have you discovered the source of the leak in your department?"

"Yes, Colonel, we think we have. It appears that one of our captains by the name of O'Bryan leaked the information. At this time I have no idea to whom or why he leaked it, but we are sure that he did it. He may have leaked it to the north end mob who have run the illegal activities throughout this city for the last fifty years. We know now that Captain O'Bryan was a dirty cop, and it appears that he made a lot of money associating with these gangsters. Besides recovering more money than I care to state, we found a journal that listed crimes that he and other members of the police department committed over the years along with the names of the mobsters who helped him and paid the police off. Finding this journal will help us clean up the department, but it tells us nothing about the Kaymark case. I suppose O'Bryan didn't have time to enter what his involvement was."

"Have you taken him into custody yet?" interrupted Small.

"Colonel, he was murdered in his apartment execution style; I would guess someone was cleaning up loose ends. So, Colonel, at this time that's the best I can give you. Most of our reliable informants aren't talking. It's very obvious that somehow the mob is involved. As yet, we have no answers and a lot of speculation."

"Maybe, Jim, I have a few things that may help you with some of your cases as well as the Kaymark case. Last year your two detectives, Ryan and Bonacursso, broke open the homicide case against Kaymark with his insurance scam. Ryan evidently realized that many of the documents and papers in Kaymark's home were in the German language. He called us and asked us to look over the material. We did, and to our amazement found a wealth of information concerning spy operations throughout the United States and Mexico as well as Central American. To tell you the truth Jim, many of the documents proved that there is a German spy operation in progress in the United States that exceeded our full knowledge of what was going on. We discovered more than forty German spies working in the United States that we had no idea were here. Jim, I am going to let you in on a little-known secret; we will be in the European war within a year. Things are moving fast in Europe; Germany is looking to start forcing all Europe under their control."

"Is there more to tell about Kaymark?"

"Yes, Jim, he was going to tell all he knew about the placement of spies and their identities—both German and our American traitors."

"Looks like we lost a well-placed source by his death."

"Not well-placed, but very knowledgeable. He could have helped us more than we will ever know in destroying the lot. We have learned quite a bit of information, as I have stated, from the Kaymark documents."

"Colonel Small, we have been overwhelmed in the last few weeks with burglaries, robberies, and property damage due to bombings and arson. We have been unable to find rhyme or reason for these felonies. Our murder rate in this city has more than doubled over the last few years. We suspect the mob is behind these crimes, but we haven't put their plot together. Maybe it's just a lot of lucky felonies they've pulled off and haven't been caught as yet. The thing that makes no sense is the apparently organized way they get their information and how organized the crimes have been. These crooks of ours in Kansas City just aren't that smart."

"Damn, Jim, here is one that you might get some teeth into! We have heard from sources that German spies have infiltrated and are working alongside your mob thugs and guiding them in the direction of many crimes being committed all over the United States. We are slowly putting the information together. As we find out some names and locations in and around Kansas City, you will be informed. Civilian police, with our aid, should be able to put an end to these people and their crimes."

Colonel Small finished his drink, shook hands, and departed the building along with O'Malley.

Chapter Thirty-two

Two weeks into the month of August, 1940, James O'Malley was again in conference with his boss, Chief of Detectives John Miller, in the Homicide Unit Office of O'Malley.

"Jim, it's been six months now since the two officers were murdered. Do you have anything new in regard to their case?"

"No, John, we really have nothing more. My detectives have done everything by the book in this case and some things under the wire to pressure informants and the mainstream gangsters in our city. We know that someone can tell us all about the incident, but no one is talking. I think, John, they are just plain more afraid of the mob than they are of us. That means it might be the top of the mob has put the word out for all of them to keep their mouths shut—or else!"

"Or else, what the hell does that mean?"

"Simple, Detective Chief . . . keep your mouth shut or we will kill you and all your family."

"Then, O'Malley, go after the top ones; the department will back you in every way."

"That means Zino Torrio.

"O'Malley, Torrio only intimidates his own people—not ours. Do you understand what I am saying, Captain?"

"I do, Detective Chief."

"How about all these bombings and assaults as well as the numerous burglaries on the government's property?"

"I've been in touch with Colonel Small of the Army Intelligence Division about the question you just asked me. His investigations have developed the probability that the Kansas City mob, again that means Zino Torrio, is behind the new wave of crime. But it is on a larger scale than we are used to."

"Jim, why would the Army know anything regarding our gangsters' activities?"

"Because they have information from numerous agencies that we are not privileged to knowing as a result of our history of corruption over the past fifty years. And as you well know, the corruption has not been weeded out to their satisfaction as yet. We have learned through Colonel Small and his trust in me that Nazi spies are guiding a lot of the crimes. While the mob is stealing, the spy group is doing sabotage and collecting information concerning our country's secrets."

"Are we ready to close the S.O.B.s down?"

"Yes, sir; I think it will be soon."

"By the way, O'Malley, the Chief just received the results of an investigation concerning you and your team of ten detectives assigned to the Central Homicide District. It seems that you and your men are completely clean."

"Thanks, Chief Miller, but I already suspected that!"

That evening O'Malley and his detectives met together at the Headquarter Homicide Office where James O'Malley discussed everything he suspected but could not prove. He gave each of his officers specific assignments to pressure the thugs into turning informants. By 0100 hours the next morning, his detectives were on the street and applying pressure concerning the more lucrative activities of the mob.

O'Malley and Walker made the decision to talk to the top mafia gangster in the Kansas City area, Zino Torrio. There was no problem in locating the man. He could always be found in his office above his bakery on St. John Street. Tonight was no exception, as he loved to gamble with old trusted friends. This way Zino always felt safe against a hit by an up-and-comer who had an eye on his position in the mob. Zino always had at least two bodyguards with him no mater where he was. He stayed away from the night clubs and never, even as a young up-and-coming Turk, did he resort to any night clubs in the mob world. He even stayed away from the notorious Chesterfield Club, which was established for the purpose of gambling and prostitution. Zino faithfully went to church every Sunday and all holidays. He took Holy Communion at early morning Mass almost every day.

He had been widowed four years earlier and wasn't known to associate with women. His one sister had married Carmine Simone. They had one child, a male, who was the apple of Zino's eye. The child was named Phil Simone. Zino had helped bring up his nephew after his father had died. Zino made sure that his nephew was brought up in the ways of a mafia prince who would some day take over the reins of the organization. The young prince had not been heard from since January. Zino quietly put out the word that he was looking for him. He had still received no information from any of his associates. Phil had just disappeared from the city. This meant that he was either hiding for some unknown reason or he was dead.

Torrio was also having trouble locating or contacting Vic Gargotta. It seemed as though Gargotta had been involved in almost every incident with the Morgan outfit. Although Gargotta was earning some big money for the outfit, he still neglected to check in as he should have been doing all along. Zino had heard from a couple of policemen that Gargotta was being diligently looked for by the police. Torrio was told that the police were after him for the armed robbery of a jewelry store in the downtown area and a shootout with the police in the northeast area of the city. The incident proved non-profitable to Gargotta and two associates were killed by police. He also heard that some of the cops chasing him had recognized him and an arrest warrant had been issued.

Chapter Thirty-three

O'Malley and Walker drove to Zino Torrio's business, located on St. John Avenue. The detectives entered through the front door of the business where they were greeted by one of the bakers at the cash wrap, as the bakery was a 24/7 operation. O'Malley then showed his badge, as did Walker. "I want to speak to Zino."

"He ain't here."

"How come his car is parked out front of the store, with a warm engine?" bluffed Walker.

The baker was caught in an embarrassing moment and could not think of a clever answer. A large man walked up to Sergeant Walker and stated, "You guys cops?"

"Yes, and I want to talk to Zino right now or I'll have twenty flatfoots searching this place, and I've never seen a cop who didn't enjoy ripping the place apart, looking for documents that would be used as evidence in some type of criminal case. I am sure your operation here will be held up for at least a full week. Then guess what."

"What?" replied the goon to O'Malley's question.

"I would be back again and do the same thing every week until I talk to your boss. Understand, shithead?"

The goon acted as though he was thinking about the consequences of not telling Zino, but decided instead that it might be real essential for him to lead the cops to his boss's office. The goon then stated, "Yes, wait here."

The mobster almost ran up the back stairs to the mafia boss's office, and as he approached the closed door, he stopped and thought exactly what he was going to say to his boss. He then knocked on Zino's door and one of Zino's bodyguards answered the knock and was told by the goon about the two detectives waiting in the bakery lobby.

The bodyguard then closed the door and walked over to Zino and informed him that there were two policemen wanting to see him. Zino looked at his gambling associates and told them he had to meet with a couple of rude cops and that his associates had better leave down the back steps and call it a night.

After all his associates had exited down the back steps, he turned to one of his bodyguards and stated, "Bring those guys up to my private office. I'll be waiting there for them."

O'Malley and Walker were led to Zino's office by a very large, powerful looking mobster. His suit was well-tailored to his body. However, you could see the outline of his shoulder holster. O'Malley estimated the weapon carried by the thug was a large caliber, probably a .45 caliber Colt semi-automatic.

Entering Zino's office, the detectives observed a second muscled thug who was dressed more casually. Both of these thugs were extremely muscular and apparently in good physical condition. The second thug wore his weapon in his waistband, not concealing the .38 revolver at all.

Zino was sitting behind his desk, looking very agitated. "What you cops want with me?" asked Zino.

"To ask you a few questions."

"What if I have no answers for you?"

"Zino, let's stop the bullshit. If you don't want to answer our questions, you can answer them at the station house instead of here in your office."

"And how do you think you are going to remove me to your station house?" asked Zino as he pointed to his two bodyguards. "I can have two more up here from downstairs if you think these two mugs can't handle your ass." Zino thought to himself that he just might be intimidating the two detectives. However, knowing O'Malley's reputation, he figured there was no way to intimidate someone like that.

"Zino, I have the greatest respect for your ability to eliminate us right here and now. But I want you to stop and think for a moment; do you think for one second my people don't know where we are, and after a certain amount of time, they will be here looking for us. And I've got to tell you, Zino, there is no doubt in my mind you will be the first they take out," stated O'Malley.

"Maybe you are bluffing, Captain."

"And maybe I'm not, Zino!"

"O'Malley, we are just talking here, I really wouldn't hurt a policeman. But why are you picking on me?"

"Right now, Zino, I only want to ask you a few questions and maybe give you some information about your people that has been kept from you."

"Like what?"

"First, Zino, I want to know when was the last time that you saw you nephew Phil Simone?"

"Why do you want to know?"

"Well, I have been looking for him for the past several months, and I know where he is if you don't."

"Well, the last time I saw my nephew or even heard anything from him was on New Year's Eve. He stopped by my office and said hello along with Vic Gargotta. I ain't seen him since."

"Why do you suppose that is?"

"How the fuck do I know! He probably got involved in some shit and is hiding out. Are you trying to tell me that you want to talk to him about some stuff? If so, I gotta tell you, I have no responsibility for what my nephew does. He's a grown man. Do you guys have a warrant for him?"

"No," replied O'Malley.

"Well then, what do you want him for?"

"To be truthful with you, Zino; I thought I wanted him for an armed robbery and a shooting."

"Well, I don't know nothing about that. But when he gets in touch with me I will tell him that you're looking for him."

"You know, Zino, if it wasn't so sad I'd laugh. But old Phil is not going to get in touch with you—ever."

"What kind of shit are you laying on me now, telling me something like that. You would think from what you say that he's not coming back—ever."

"That's what I'm telling you."

There was a long pause before Zino even attempted to speak. "Was my nephew indicted in another state?"

"No, Zino, he wasn't indicted in another state. In fact, he never left Kansas City. Zino, your nephew is dead and his body was destroyed and dumped by two of your black constituents at the request of Vic Gargotta after he was killed in a gambling game at a Negro bar."

Zino's faced turned ashen and his eyes started to water as he tried to speak. His voice was choked. "O'Malley, you're saying that my nephew was murdered and Vic Gargotta was with him."

"Yes, that is absolutely correct, except it was probably self-defense on the part of the shooter as your nephew had pulled a gun and threatened to shoot him. Now I know this is a shock to you and I know how you felt about your nephew, but I think you need to know that Vic Gargotta betrayed you by not telling you and attempting to keep it from you. I want to speak to Gargotta; do you know where he is at this time?"

"No, I do not know where he is. I have heard that he is running with a bunch of Irish gangsters out of the Boston area. But I will put out word that I want to talk to him and send him right down to see you."

O'Malley laughed to himself and looked at Walker, thinking if Zino lives up to his reputation Gargotta is going to be eliminated. After a few more questions, O'Malley and Walker excused themselves and were escorted out through the bakery onto the sidewalk, where they entered their unmarked police vehicle and started driving away.

"What do you think, Jim? Are we gonna find Gargotta in some alley, cause you know Zino is going to knock him off as revenge and for disloyalty."

"What we're gonna do is watch Zino and his bodyguards for the next couple of days, cause I know they know where he is. And if I know Zino, he will want to confront Gargotta himself and do the execution Italian style."

Chapter Thirty-four

Zino sat in his office at his desk, apparently lost in his thoughts. Was the detective telling the truth about his nephew? If he was, and Gargotta knew about it, he had failed to let him know about the demise of his relative, then what else was Gargotta holding out from him? Zino knew the reputation of Captain James O'Malley, and therefore suspected that everything the detective said about the death of his nephew was true.

When Zino's bodyguards returned, he asked them both point-blank if they had heard anything in regards to his nephew. Both of the goons indicated that they had not heard anything about him. Zino, with a sadness that neither of the thugs understood, ordered the two to locate Vic Gargotta. However, he did not want them to let Gargotta know that he was interested in his whereabouts or his activities. If they came in contact with him, they were to let Gargotta know that Zino wanted to see him—nothing more.

O'Malley and Walker set up a surveillance on both of Zino's bodyguards, hoping that they might lead them to Gargotta. Walker also contacted Detectives Ryan and Bonacursso, who would assist with the surveillance of the two thugs. O'Malley thought that Zino wouldn't personally look for Gargotta, instead he would rely on his bodyguards to locate him, thus not leading the police to find

Gargotta. Detective Ryan and his partner Phil Bonacursso both sat on a surveillance of the bakery. They had been at that location approximately one hundred yards from the entrance to the bakery, where they could see both the front and rear entrances to the establishment, as well as the comings and goings of the employees and their deliveries. Approximately two hours into the surveillance, the two detectives observed Gino Campo, the largest of Zino's bodyguards. This guy was so big and muscular that he was easy to spot six blocks away from wherever he was standing. They watched Gino walk out of the building and enter a black ford two-door. He started out of the parking area onto the street; at that time Detective Ryan radioed O'Malley that they were following Gino Campo and gave the description of the vehicle he was driving.

O'Malley and Walker remained at the front of the bakery, approximately one block west of the entrance. As they observed the storefront, they noticed that numerous known gangsters, both of the Italian mob and many that the police thought were lone wolf type criminals, were going in and out of the bakery, but upon leaving appeared not to have purchased anything. So it was guessed that they were there to talk with Zino about mob business.

Meanwhile, Ryan and Bonacursso followed Gino Campo to the west side of the city, known as the central industrial area. Gino drove to a large seven-story warehouse with a sign stating it was Acme Storage. Gino parked his vehicle, then walked into the building.

"Shall we follow him in?" asked Ryan.

"Hell, yes; I wouldn't be surprised if Vic Gargotta was hiding somewhere inside. Both Bonacursso and Ryan entered the building on foot in an attempt to follow Gino and see if he made contact with Vic Gargotta.

O'Malley observed Zino, along with his other bodyguard, exit the front door of the bakery. The bodyguard looked both up and down the street, then motioned to the driver of an automobile parked one hundred feet from the bakery. The driver pulled the vehicle up in front of the bakery; both Zino and his bodyguard positioned themselves in the rear seat of the car. The vehicle then moved swiftly down the street with O'Malley and Walker following.

Ryan and Bonacursso both entered the building, and as they did, the sickening smell of slaughtered animals and their remains were ripe and made them gag as they took their first breaths. Bonacursso felt as if he were going to vomit. The two detectives moved quickly through the interior of the first floor where they encountered numerous employees of what appeared to be a meatpacking plant. No one challenged the detectives' presence in the building. They walked up the stairs to the second floor where they could hear two men talking to each other in Italian. As Bonacursso listened, he heard Gino tell someone that Zino wanted to meet him later today at his office. He also told the other person that the police were also looking for him, so he had better be very careful. Gino then did a little chitchatting with the other man, then told him, "I'll be seeing you." Gino then left and walked out of the office and took a freight elevator down to the first floor.

"Joe, I am sure he was talking to Vic Gargotta, and he must still be in that office. What do you want to do?" asked Bonacursso.

"We might not get another chance to arrest him, so I say we take him now."

"Sounds good to me, Joe."

"O.K., Phil, I will go in first, weigh the situation, and you watch my back."

Both detectives were on opposite sides of the doorway. Ryan crouched low with his service revolver at the ready, as did Bonacursso. Ryan opened the door to reveal a dimly lit office area. Ryan rushed in and found it empty. A quick search revealed an exit from the office towards the back. As Gargotta hadn't passed the detectives and had not used the elevator, they suspected he had used the stairway going up to the next floor by going through the exit door in the back.

The detectives followed their suspicions and ascended the stairs to the next level, where the lighting was brighter, revealing the third floor to be a massive storage area for furniture and other office equipment. Ryan stepped in and positioned himself next to the wall, listening for any sounds. As he listened and adjusted his eyes to the lighting, he noticed what he thought was a shadow of a man about thirty yards to his left. As Bonacursso stepped into the storage area, he also observed the shadow of a man, except the shadow became a man by the name of Vic Gargotta. He was holding a 12-gauge pump shotgun.

Chapter Thirty-five

O'Malley and Walker followed Zino and his bodyguard as his driver drove through the city. O'Malley had observed that Zino had his vehicle run stop signs, make U-turns, and drive around the same block several times in an attempt to catch a glimpse of anyone trying to follow them. Zino, after an hour of this activity, must have been satisfied there was no one following him as they continued to the downtown area, where Zino, without his bodyguard, was let out in front of the Aladdin Hotel. The bodyguard and driver parked two blocks down the street and waited. O'Malley parked his police vehicle, and with Walker in tow, walked into the lobby of the Aladdin Hotel. They identified themselves to the lobby manager, and they asked if he had seen Zino and where he went. The manager informed the detectives that the only person of that description to enter had gone into the bar, which was pretty crowded at this time of the evening.

O'Malley and Walker entered the lounge, and to their surprise, saw numerous patrons who were waiting for a table. Both officers walked to the bar and found Zino at a table with three other men. They had ordered a meal and appeared to be waiting for it to arrive. They were engaged in what appeared to be friendly conversation.

"I would give a month's pay to know what they are talking about and who the other three men are. Have you ever seen them before, John?"

"No," replied Walker.

"But I have," stated a familiar voice behind O'Malley, who had apparently been listening to them without their knowledge.

O'Malley turned, as did Walker, and found the voice to belong to Colonel Small of the Army Intelligence Unit. Colonel Small greeted both O'Malley and Walker with a smile and a handshake, then stated, "I have a table located over in the corner. We can watch them from there and talk in some privacy."

After being seated, Colonel Small asked who the newcomer to the party was. "I'm surprised you don't know him; that's Zino Torrio, mob boss here in Kansas City," answered O'Malley.

"So that's what he looks like; he's not so tough looking in person, is he?"

"Don't fool yourself; he is one smart, mean, scary guy," replied Walker.

"Now, Small, who are the other three?" asked O'Malley.

"First off, the one who looks like a Boston lawyer is a professor of law at the Harvard University. He has been living at this hotel for the past four months. He was brought to our attention by a file found in the Kaymark home. This file indicated he was somehow involved in and with German intelligence. Other sources we have developed say he is a spy for Germany. We have been keeping close tabs on this guy and are sure he is involved in a lot of the sabotage happening around the metro area as well as the highjacking of a lot of freight on trains and trucks. We have had taps on his telephone and in his apartment for weeks now and have learned that the other two men with him are German agents. We now know who they are and why they are here. It appears they are constantly attending meetings of American/German organizations, and we have observed them meeting with Nazi sympathizers. The dandy professor's name is Peter Morgan. How about that; he took a Jewish name for cover. Our sources said all of that bunch are stone-cold killers. From our taps, we suspect Morgan and another man probably associated with your guy Zino, were the ones who masterminded the hit on Kaymark after it was discovered he was going to supply us with information. O'Malley, we want to catch all of them together in a crime so that we can put them behind bars. Otherwise, we do have people who will eliminate them if that's the way we have to go."

"Son of a bitch, Colonel, your people don't play games, do they?"

"No, O'Malley, we don't; and we do not play by the same rules that you have to. We protect the United States against those who might destroy us."

O'Malley observed Zino in what appeared to be a heated and intense argument with Morgan. In typical Italian gestures, Zino was making his case, and it appeared that Morgan was not laying back and taking his mouth. Apparently they noticed people watching them, therefore they quieted down and continued their conversation in lowered voices.

"O'Malley, we should have some nice information on Morgan and his associates before long. I will give you everything we find," said Colonel Small.

"Thanks," O'Malley stated.

Chapter Thirty-six

Detectives Ryan and Bonacursso each rolled to the left and right sides at the same time, hitting the floor hard while Gargotta fired his shotgun where the detectives had been.

Ryan fired two wild shots, just missing his target. While both detectives ran for cover, Gargotta then ran for an exit door while firing his second shot, which struck Ryan in the left arm, knocking him to the ground. Gargotta then ran out the exit and to the steps, where he hid behind a container, waiting for the detectives to walk out the door. Bonacursso, realizing that Ryan had been hit, ran to where he was laying. "How bad are you hit, Joe?"

"That fuck hit me in the left shoulder and hand, and I think there's a pellet in the calf of my leg. Otherwise, I am O.K., Phil. Go get that cocksucker."

"You bet I will!"

"Be sure to carefully open that exit door. As soon as I get the bleeding stopped, I'll join you."

Bonacursso ran to the exit door, dropped to his knees, and pushed open the door. Two fast shots rang out and splintered the wooden door and its frame, causing wooden debris to fly in the air and drop in splinters around the detective. Bonacursso shot three rapid shots at the area where he thought the suspect was. The detective then rolled into the hallway just in time to see Gargotta running up the stairs. Bonacursso fired one round at Gargotta, grazing his calf. Gargotta yelled out in pain, but continued on his way up the stairs to the roof door, which he opened, then turned and fired his shotgun down the stairs at the detective. Gargotta then ran onto the roof, limping as the pain increased in his left leg. He made it across the roof and into the shadows and dropped to the tar roof floor behind a chimney where he waited. Bonacursso cautiously walked through the roof's door onto the roof floor. Bonacursso yelled, "Gargotta, give it up; you have nowhere to go."

"Fuck you, cop; I'll kill you before the night is over."

"Gargotta, you sure talk tough for a fucking coward." Bonacursso strained his eyes to locate the gangster.

"Come and get me, cop, if you think you can."

Bonacursso thought he knew from the sounds of the gangster's voice where he was hiding. But he was unable to see him to take a shot. As he had not reloaded, he had only one bullet left in his revolver.

"Say, Detective; what's your fucking name anyway."

"Why," replied Bonacursso.

"I want to know the name of the cop I'm going to kill. I didn't know the names of the two I killed in the northeast area of the city. If I had, I would have sent the sons-of-bitches flowers to their funerals."

"Are you telling me you are the one who murdered the two policemen on Belmont Street a few months ago?"

"Yes, and you ain't any smarter than they were. They died because they were chasing me. And here you are, doing the same goddamn thing."

Bonacursso silently moved closer to what appeared to be a black chimney.

"Tell me your name, detective, so I can personally tell your family members how brave you were before I killed you."

"It's Bonacursso, asshole."

Bonacursso was about five feet from where Gargotta's voice seemed to be coming.

"I've heard of you, Detective. You're supposed to be one smart cop. Let's just see how smart you are. I've got ten grand stashed away that I'll make sure you get if you back off and let me go."

"Shit, Gargotta, where would you get that much money?"

"Easy, cop; I got it off a pig Captain of your department. I had to cut his throat to get it, but I'll tell you, he's probably just like you—a dirty cop who needed killing. Hell, I did the department and the public a favor by knocking that fat pig off."

Bonacursso took another step closer to the gangster, and in doing so, made the slightest scuff noise with his shoes. He stopped moving and hoped Gargotta hadn't heard the noise. That was a mistake, as the gangster knew the detective was standing directly in front of his hiding place.

The gangster jumped up, aimed the shotgun, and pulled the trigger, only to realize his weapon was empty. Bonacursso fired his gun at the same time, hitting the shotgun's stock. Gargotta then swung the shotgun at the detective, striking him in the chest and knocking him to the ground. The gangster was now striking at Bonacursso's head. He missed, but continued to advance on him with deadly rage. Bonacursso threw his empty revolver at Gargotta, striking him in the head, which slowed the gangster down. Gargotta dropped his shotgun, then pulled a switchblade knife from his pocket and again advanced on the detective, swinging and stabbing at the officer, cutting his face and kicking the policeman while he was on the ground. Upon hitting the ground, Bonacursso rolled to his left, kicking out at Gargotta, striking his wounded leg. The gangster then fell on the detective and attempted to stab him in the chest. The battle continued as they both rolled over and over. Somehow Bonacursso had turned the knife around on Gargotta and plunged it into his chest to the hilt. The fight, at that moment, went out of the gangster and he lay dead on Bonacursso.

Detective Ryan limped through the roof door with his weapon in his hand. Looking at Bonacursso and Gargotta, he asked, "Is the asshole dead, Phil?"

"Yes."

"Good, now let's get some medical help. I can't get this goddamned bleeding stopped!"

Chapter Thirty-seven

As O'Malley and Walker returned to their squad car, O'Malley received a radio call to respond to the city hospital on an injured detective. He heard the dispatcher contact Detective Croix to respond to a stabbing at a warehouse in the central industrial area of the city. The dispatcher also informed Detective Croix that "officers were involved". The dispatcher then notified O'Malley of the same information. O'Malley stopped at a pay phone and called the police dispatcher, who filled him in on all the information he had concerning the stabbing call.

"Who are the officers involved?"

"Seems to be Detectives Ryan and Bonacursso. Ryan was wounded with a gunshot and Bonacursso had several cuts to his face and neck."

"Do you know the name of the deceased?"

"Not yet; we are waiting on Detective Croix to notify us. Are you responding to the scene?'

"No; I am sending Sergeant Walker. I am going to the hospital to check on the officers involved." O'Malley hung up the phone and returned to his vehicle, where he filled Sergeant Walker in on the situation. He informed Walker that he was sending him to the scene to supervise, and he would meet Detective Croix there. Then O'Malley went on to inform Walker that O'Malley would drop

Walker off at the scene. When finished, he was to respond back to the office with Detective Croix. In the meantime, O'Malley would check on the injured officers at the hospital.

When O'Malley got to the hospital he was admitted to Ryan's room, which was located on the third floor. Ryan was scheduled for surgery on his left shoulder and foot, where he had been struck by the shotgun pellets. Ryan was under sedation and not making much sense. Ryan was able to speak to O'Malley for a few seconds before he drifted off into a dream world. O'Malley then went to the emergency room where he found Detective Bonacursso lying on a gurney being stitched up by a doctor.

"Huh, looks like you will be sporting more scars, Phil."

"Hey, Captain, looks that way, don't it?"

"Feel like telling me what happened," asked O'Malley.

Phil Bonacursso then told O'Malley the entire story.

"Phil, you are sure he stated that he killed the two police officers, Toller and Smith, as well as Captain O'Bryan?"

"Yes."

"Did he mention whether or not he killed the gangster Candanza?"

"No, boss, he didn't, but I think that's why he was running from Officers Toller and Smith in the first place. I also think Toller and Smith had no idea that Gargotta had just killed Candanza."

"I agree with you, Phil. Did he mention killing O'Bryan by name?"

"No, he didn't; but who else would he be talking about?"

"I suspect you are correct on that also. Did he mention who he worked for on the killings?"

"No, he didn't; but Captain, we both know it is Zino Torrio that he works for."

"I'm afraid you're right again, Phil."

"How is Joe doing, Captain?"

"They are taking him to surgery. I've had a district car pick up his wife and bring her to the hospital. That reminds me, I had better meet her when she arrives. I'll see you later, Phil. And Phil, by the way, good job."

147

O'Malley walked out of the emergency room and back up to the room of Joe Ryan in order to be there when Ryan's wife arrived.

Later in the day, O'Malley returned to his office where Walker and Robert Croix were finishing up their reports. He spoke to them for a few moments, and excused himself to call the Chief of Detectives. "John, this is O'Malley. We have gotten a few breaks on a couple of cases." O'Malley went on to explain the day's events and the unsolicited confession of Gargotta before he died.

"So, we have solved all four murders with Gargotta being the perpetrator?"

"That seems to be the story and the end of the case as far as the public is concerned."

"James, as soon as I notify the Chief, I want you to release what information you think is necessary to satisfy the press. And, by the way, who are the two detectives who have been injured and how are they doing?" asked the Chief of Detectives.

"Ryan had surgery and will do fine, but will be in the hospital for a few days. Then he will be on administrative leave until he's healed. Detective Bonacursso has been stitched up and released from the hospital. He will be back at work in a few days."

"Be sure and give both of these men a lot of credit in the press for an outstanding job. I will notify the Chief of the events and he will want to make a personal appearance at the hospital to visit with the wounded officer. And, by the way, James, that's a job well done."

O'Malley read the reports that had been placed on his desk and approved them. He then set up a press conference for 9:00 p.m. with the newsmen. O'Malley then sat back in his desk chair and sighed to himself. He was glad the homicides of Toller and Smith had been cleared and Gargotta was out of the way permanently. It was now December 6, 1941, eight months since the murders. O'Malley was going home to get some rest.

Chapter Thirty-eight

O'Malley, after the press conference, felt extremely exhausted. He returned to his office and signed out for the night and then headed home. Arriving home, he took a shower and then poured himself a good, stiff drink of bourbon. It was almost 1:00 a.m. when he finally fell into his bed and into a sound sleep. At four a.m., O'Malley's telephone started ringing. It took O'Malley a few moments to bring himself awake enough to answer the phone. "Hello," snorted O'Malley.

"Sorry to wake you, but I just heard your press conference on the radio and wanted to congratulate you on the job you and your men have done. What I want to know is if you want to finish the job."

"Who is this?" asked O'Malley.

"Damn, James; I was hoping I made a lasting impression when last we met. It's Colonel Small."

"Sorry, Colonel," O'Malley stated with a sarcastic yawn. "I was sound asleep when you called. What in the hell is on your mind at this hour?"

"I repeat my question. How would you like to be in on the arrest of Zino Torrio for theft of government property and sabotage, along with the arrests of four very bad German spies?"

"Hell, yes, I would. When and where?"

"We want to get them early, and I mean early—like in the morning. I have agents of mine on all the main players; that way none escape our raids. Can you and your team be ready by 0600 hours?"

"Yes."

"Good, James. I'll meet you at your office, and by the way, inform Sergeant Walker I like my coffee fresh, hot and black."

"I will, Colonel, and thanks for the invite."

By 0600 hours, O'Malley, Walker and Detective Croix, along with the wounded Detective Bonacursso, were in O'Malley's office waiting for Colonel Small. Sergeant Walker and Detective Croix both were reading the Kansas City newspaper regarding O'Malley's press release. The article was actually praising the detectives and the police department for solving four murders which all appeared, according to the press, to be gang-related, as well as clearing the case of the three murdered police officers. The press seemed extremely pleased in their sensational coverage of the termination of the killer Gargotta. The fact that it made headlines on the front page really impressed the police officers as they read the account.

"Jesus, both Ryan and Bonacursso are fucking heroes now in the newspapers," stated Robert Croix.

"I'd bet neither of their hats will fit them now," stated Sergeant Walker with a loud belly laugh.

"From the account you and Croix recapped in your report, I must admit they are true heroes of our department. I will bet you money that within a month our two heroes will be on the cover of at least "True Detective" and "True Crime" magazines. However, knowing those two, I will bet money that the story will be wildly embellished for their readers," laughed O'Malley.

"Say, Walker, Colonel Small wanted me to tell you that he likes his coffee fresh, hot and black."

"Oh, fuck him; the coffee is already made and waiting."

Shortly, Colonel Small and ten of his agents arrived at the Homicide Unit where they gathered in the squad office and were introduced to the homicide detectives. Colonel Small singled out

Detective Bonacursso to all of his agents as one of the detectives that first put them onto Kaymark's case and killed, most likely, the son-of-a-bitch who ambushed the military escort along with Kaymark. The other party or parties involved may be one of the bastards they intend to arrest today.

O'Malley's telephone rang five times before Sergeant John Walker answered it. He listened for a moment, and then put the phone down. "Colonel Small, the telephone call is for you."

"Thanks, Sergeant." He then answered the telephone call. After a brief conversation, Colonel Small informed O'Malley and the rest of the gathering, "I have just received some bad news, the Japanese attacked the United States early this morning, severely damaging our naval fleet and base at Pearl Harbor, Hawaii." There was stunned silence in the room. Colonel Small continued, "I suspect by this evening we will be at war. Therefore, I will now tell you why we are going to arrest the individuals on this list I am handing out to each of you. The people on this list are known spies, criminals, and enemies of the United States. As such, 'due process' is discontinued where these names are listed. Be advised, they may all be armed. Some of them, we know, are stone cold killers and will not hesitate to shoot and kill any of you. Some are only involved to make money. Whatever the reason, we want them. Upon arrest of anyone on this list, they will be turned over, either dead or alive, to me and my people. You police detectives will recognize many names of your city's criminal element. Your assignment will be to arrest them and bring them to your jail."

"Holy shit, Zino Torrio is on this list, as well as some of his men," stated Detective Croix.

"Yes, detective, and Captain O'Malley will be in charge of those underworld gangsters who are captured. I also have felony warrants for each name of the list. There are five Germans on the list who are here in the United States illegally. My men know them and will pick them up one way or another."

The Colonel talked for about twenty more minutes and then told all the agents and officers gathered there that he and Captain O'Malley will give the assignments out and control all activities from the command post in the homicide squad room. At this time James O'Malley gave his detectives five names to be arrested and brought to the city jail, booked, then turned over to Colonel Small.

Colonel Small gave his men their assignments and let them leave to locate their targets.

O'Malley asked Small if there was any other information on the attacks at Pearl Harbor.

"I can only tell you what they have told me, James; the attack is bad."

"When will it be released to the American public?"

"I suspect it will be in this evening's news—both newspapers and radio."

Sergeant Walker and Detective Robert Croix were teamed together. Detective Phil Bonacursso was to remain with Captain O'Malley as a recorder of events as they came in, as well as making sure that all of the investigators, when they made arrests, completed their reports and forwarded them to O'Malley for processing and distribution to Colonel Small and the Chief of Detectives. Both the Chief of Police and the Chief of Detectives were made aware of the targets and why they would be arrested. O'Malley had the complete confidence of the police department's heads to handle this operation.

By 11:00 a.m., Colonel Small's people were bringing in numerous thugs on the list, but were unable to locate Peter Morgan and his four associates. Zino Torrio was also nowhere to be found. Around 10:00 p.m., Colonel Small and his men returned to the police headquarters to process their earlier arrests. Detective Sergeant Walker, along with Detective Croix, continued looking for Zino Torrio. Some of the captured thugs told Walker and Croix that Zino had left town and was traveling to a hideout somewhere in southern Missouri or Arkansas. Others had informed that Zino was hiding here in Kansas City. No one really had any idea of where Morgan and his associates had disappeared to.

There were forty-one names on the gangster list that O'Malley was holding in his hand. Of the forty-one, they had arrested thirty-six and were now ready to turn over all of the thirty-six to Colonel Small for transportation by the military police on a bus to Fort Leavenworth Penitentiary for further investigation and charges against the government. You can be assured the bus was well-protected.

Chapter Thirty-nine

For the next ninety days O'Malley and his crew, as well as Colonel Small and his agents, diligently searched for the five missing people without any contact or information concerning their whereabouts. Colonel Small sent a nationwide alert for these people as listed spies and saboteurs loose upon the United States. This pickup order was also extended to all police agencies throughout the United States.

On the fourth month of searching for these individuals, Colonel Small contacted O'Malley by phone and stated, "Believe it or not, I have a location on Zino Torrio. According to a source, he has a mansion located just east of Independence, Missouri, on Highway 24. Our source stated that he is sure that Peter Morgan and his associates are also staying at that mansion. As soon as they send a reconnaissance squad to investigate the exact location, and if, indeed, any of those five are at that location, he would notify O'Malley and they would both put teams together to apprehend those individuals."

"That's fine," stated O'Malley in a very excited manner, as he thoroughly wanted to bring these bastards to justice one way or the other.

Chapter Forty

It was now early February, 1941. Colonel Small had contact with O'Malley in the Chief of Police Office. In attendance was the Chief and John Miller along with Captain James O'Malley and Detective Sergeant John Walker. Colonel Small was addressing the gathered group of police officers and his special agents who were in attendance regarding the location of Zino Torrio, Peter Morgan, and Morgan's three associates.

"We have located the house containing the five criminals that we really want to apprehend just east of Independence, Missouri. The house is off of Highway 24 on an 800-acre tract of land. There are about 70 cows in the pasture area at that location. These fugitives are living in an antebellum type house; we know very little about the house structure. We found no records of the architecture. What we do know is that the structure is a two-story with a massive porch on both the downstairs and the upstairs. These two porches completely surround the structure. The front doors are massive as well as the back doors. The house appears to have floor-to-ceiling style windows, as you would see in the plantations in Louisiana and Georgia. The front contains six massive pillars worked into the structure. These windows appear to be the type that would open up as would a large door. This would allow numerous escape exits from the structure. The structure cannot be approached by vehicle without letting the occupants know we are approaching. Therefore, we will drive to a certain point where a group of trees will cover our vehicles, and that's where we will park the automobiles. We will unload at that location and approach the fugitive's structure on foot."

"How many vehicles will we take and how many men?" asked Sergeant Walker.

"Five sedans, four men to a car, that will be twenty men, loaded with rifles and side arms. Of these rifles, four are Browning automatic rifles, five .303 Springfields, and the rest are 12-guage Winchester shotguns, pump-style. The side arms will be .38 caliber normal police issue. Believe me, gentlemen, we will be well armed," stated Colonel Small.

"What are the chances of gun play?" asked the Chief of Police.

"Chief, I think it will be their choice if gun play happens, but I am certainly hoping that this plan will eliminate any gun play, as we should be able to take them by surprise," answered Colonel Small.

"Have the other law enforcement, such as the county and state police, been notified of our intentions to arrest these felons?" questioned the Police Chief.

"Yes, sir, they have; they will be our backup and they will be standing by in a field about three miles away from the target house."

"Is there anyone else living in this home?" asked O'Malley.

"Yes, there is a caretaker and his wife who live approximately one hundred yards from the target house on the north side. It is our intention that they will be held at their home by some of my men," answered the colonel.

"Are there any other structures we need to be aware of?" asked O'Malley.

"Yes, James, there are two large barns east of the main house and a couple of storage structures northwest of the barns. I have men who will secure those buildings before we enter the main house. I have maps that have been drawn up by my people of the area layout, which we will go over very soon. Each officer involved in this event will be given a copy of the map."

It was a cold, wet morning, and snow was on the ground from a storm the day before. The temperature stood at fifteen degrees with a western wind of twenty-five miles an hour that was fierce and biting. Colonel Small, O'Malley, and their men were waiting inside an abandoned barn about four miles from the antebellum hideout of Zino Torrio and his German associates. Colonel Small ordered all present to the center of the barn where he had parked his military vehicle. Small spread out a large map of the area and distributed smaller maps to each officer and special agent involved in this apprehension. He then went over the map completely and gave each man their particular assignment. The first two special agents would cut the telephone lines to the property, then return for another assignment; four agents were dispatched to check the structures on the farm for any surprises and to physically take out any obstructions to the assault on the targeted structure. Two special agents were sent to round up the caretakers. It was 0230 hours on this cold morning and dark as hell. It was too cloudy to see the stars or the moon. However, this would make easier concealment for the law enforcement officers to approach all the structures in stealth and total concealment.

"We will have to walk to our target destination in this weather, gentlemen, and I kid you not; it is colder than a well digger's ass. So I imagine this will be a new experience to most of you law enforcement officers," said Colonel Small.

"I hope everyone has dressed appropriately," O'Malley joked with a hearty laugh.

"I'm sure they have, Jim, 'cause if they didn't they're going to freeze to death," stated Colonel Small and started laughing.

"By 0330 hours all officers were in position and had cut the telephone lines and searched the barns and other structures. The caretaker and his wife had been routed from their bed and the special agents had explained about the raid on the main house and why it was being conducted. Both were allowed to remain in their house under the guard of two of the military agents. The agents had learned from the caretaker that the property was owned by a couple of politicians and a lawyer out of Kansas City as an investment. The caretaker also told the agents that the men inside were all armed, as they were supposed to be hunters up from Kansas City. The men had been here for at least two weeks and, according to the caretaker, they had never participated in any hunting on this farm. Upon learning this information, one of the agents walked to Colonel Small's location and informed him and Captain O'Malley of the information he had learned. The special agent was then ordered to return to the caretaker's home until told otherwise.

Colonel Small, along with O'Malley and the other men, was now making the approach to the two-story target structure. O'Malley and Walker approached the front of the house, running at full speed. As they approached the front steps they slowed down slightly and, as quietly as they could, climbed the steps to the front porch, where they checked the front door and all the windows. Both officers found that all the windows and doors in their area of approach had been secured by interior locking. They listened for any sound from inside and heard none; however, the wind was creating a severe howling sound that would not allow the officers to hear any sound from the interior.

Colonel Small joined O'Malley and Walker as O'Malley pulled a set of lock picks from his trouser pocket and then started working on the front door. After a few moments O'Malley had the door unlocked. O'Malley was then joined by Detective Robert Croix and three other special agents of the military. O'Malley motioned for the other men to enter the front of the house along with O'Malley and Small. As they entered, they found themselves in a large foyer. O'Malley pointed Colonel Small and two special agents to search the downstairs while O'Malley and his men searched the upstairs area.

Colonel Small, while checking the two back bedrooms in the very rear of the house, noticed both bedrooms had luggage stacked and unopened. The beds had been left in disarray, as though recently slept in. But the occupants had left in a hurry. At that moment, the Colonel realized that the suspects who had been sleeping downstairs must have awakened and went either downstairs to the basement area or upstairs. If either one of these were the case, Colonel Small was certain that the suspects had been alerted somehow and were waiting to ambush the detectives as they walked to the second floor.

Small heard the rapid fire of .38 caliber revolvers and then the distinct sound of a Browning automatic rifle being fired in what sounded to be the upper area of the house.

The gun battle stopped as suddenly as it started, with three men lying dead or in the process of dying, on the upper floor area. One was dying in the stairwell.

Later, when Captain O'Malley made out his recap of the incident to the Chief of Detectives, he wrote that as Sergeant Walker, Detective Croix, and himself were in the process of climbing the staircase, a man later identified as a German agent, charged down the steps firing an automatic rifle. Gunfire was returned by his detectives and himself, hitting the gunman, who later died. As the detectives continued up the stairs they were again fired upon by two more gunmen armed with .45 caliber pistols. These men were shortly dispatched. One lay dead on the second floor and the other lay dead behind him.

A complete search of the house revealed no more suspects. It appeared, if their information was correct, that Zino and Morgan had fled the house while the gun battle ensued. Neither were found; however, upon a more thorough search they found a secret passageway that led to a shed approximately one-half mile from the target house. At that location, automobile tracks were discovered and followed until they entered the highway.

The Army handled all of the crime scene as our officers were involved in the shooting.

Late that night, O'Malley and his crew returned to the homicide office in Kansas City, where O'Malley filled his boss, Chief of Detectives Miller, in on the events at the plantation site. Miller, in turn, notified the Chief while O'Malley and his crew of detectives wrote up their respective reports.

Chapter Forty-one

The following week found Sergeant Walker and Captain O'Malley on a surveillance at Zino Torrio's bakery with the hope that Zino might show up. It was 1000 hours, the sky was dark gray, and it was eight degrees above zero. There was no real wind to be noticed and no traffic on the street.

Sergeant Walker was doing his best to keep the windows on the automobile from icing up. O'Malley looked over at Walker, then stated, "John, one thing I have learned about this city and it's crime elements—they are nothing more than a breed of city wolves who are always on the lookout for something to prey on."

"Yes, James, but look at it this way; we are the hunters of those city wolves."

Detectives Bonacursso and Croix were now teamed up and assigned to check all of Zino's properties and hangouts. They spent the entire day searching the city. In the evening, they picked up carryout food, drove to Detective Joe Ryan's home, and shared supper with him. They informed Joe of all the activity in and around the unit since he had been hospitalized. They found that Ryan's wounds were healing well and he couldn't wait to get back to work. They talked much about the war and what the papers were saying about it.

O'Malley and Walker had no better luck with their surveillance than Bonacursso and Croix had. They called it a night and headed home. Although the city was snowed in, windy, and cold, crimes were continuous throughout the city: murder, assault, and burglaries all continued at a steady pace. Extortion, property damage, robberies, arsons; it seemed like the crimes never stopped, no matter what the weather was like. Neither was the police department deterred, and the apprehensions of criminals continued.

Two uniformed officers in a patrol car were in a snow covered alleyway checking the back of the businesses in their area of assignment.

The patrol unit drove over something across the alleyway hidden by the snow. The driver stopped the automobile and looked at his partner, stating, "What the fuck was that?"

His partner replied, "Damned if I know. Probably some litterbug dumped a rolled up carpet."

The driver and his partner exited their patrol car to check for damages to the vehicle. They found none, but did find what they had run over. It was a white male with four nice neat bullet holes into his chest. The driver looked more closely at the corpse and his face and stated, "I think I know who this is."

"Who?" asked his partner.

"Zino Torrio."

"The gangster?"

"Yes, exactly."

"Are you shitting me?" he asked as his partner looked closer at the dead man's face. "Jesus Christ, we'd better call the sergeant!"

Within a few hours Captain O'Malley, Sergeant Walker, and Detective Phil Bonacursso along with Patrol Sergeant George Mints were standing around the body of Zino Torrio, waiting for a coroner's wagon to remove the corpse to the morgue. O'Malley assigned Bonacursso and his partner, Robert Croix, to complete the crime scene investigation, then respond to the morgue to see what the medical examiner had to reveal in his investigation.

O'Malley left Walker to help with the crime scene while he returned to the homicide office. Once there, O'Malley contacted

Colonel Small by telephone and informed him that Zino had been found shot to death in an alley early that morning.

"Anything on Morgan?" asked Small.

"No, I was hoping to hear something from you."

"James, we haven't heard anything on Morgan since we had it out with his associates at the plantation house."

"Keep me up to date," stated O'Malley. He then hung up the telephone.

Later that afternoon, Bonacursso phoned O'Malley from the morgue and reported that the autopsy revealed that Zino had been shot four times in the chest. Any one of the shots would have caused his death.

"Anything else, Phil?"

"Yes, Zino was in full winter gear when shot—overcoat, grey suit, and buckle up galoshes, which I guess could mean he was shot in the alleyway where we found him."

"Thanks, Phil. Keep me posted if you discover anything else."

"I will, boss. Oh, I almost forgot; street rumors have it that Salvatore DiMaggio is already the new don here in Kansas City. I'll bet those guys knew about Zino's demise way before the body was discovered."

"You can take that to the bank, Phil."

Across the state line in Kansas City, Kansas, Morgan was sitting in a safe house that he had set up for just such an occasion—if anything had gone wrong and he needed an escape route.

Since Zino Torrio was now wanted by both the police and the military, Zino needed to be eliminated before he was caught by either organization. Therefore, Morgan contacted Zino's number two man, a mean little gangster by the name of DiMaggio, who was ambitious and ready to move to the top of the underworld of Kansas City. DiMaggio received a telephone call from Zino, commanding him to pick Torrio up in the alleyway a few blocks from his home. When DiMaggio arrived, he found Zino waiting in the alleyway in front of the rear entry to a clothing store. Zino walked toward DiMaggio's vehicle; DiMaggio stepped out of his car, shot Zino four times in the chest with a .357 Magnum, killing Zino instantly.

DiMaggio then re-entered his automobile and casually drove off into the snow and the deserted roadway. Morgan, after receiving information that Zino was dead, made some long-distance phone calls and set up his escape later than evening by train.

O'Malley received a telephone call from the Chief of Detectives, John Miller, who informed him that the Chief of Police wanted him to report to his office without delay. The Chief of Detectives further advised O'Malley that he would be there also.

O'Malley was shown into the Chief's Office where the Chief of Detectives, John Miller, along with two Police Commissioners, were sitting at a large rectangular table. O'Malley noticed that a thick folder was in front of the Chief. O'Malley realized that it was his employee folder; all documents concerning his activities in the police department were in that file.

The Chief introduced O'Malley to the two Police Commissioners. At this time a few of the city leaders walked into the office and were introduced to the tabled group. They took a seat at the table also. Coffee was served to all by the Chief's aide, Police Officer Jack Hunter. While the assembled men were enjoying their coffee, two more men entered the Chief's office. O'Malley recognized both; the first was the Governor of the State of Missouri along with O'Malley's friend Colonel Small of Military Intelligence. The Chief introduced all present to the newest arrivals.

After all present had their coffee, the Chief stood and stated, "Today is a very sad day for me personally as we have to say goodbye to an outstanding policeman and administrator as well as my good friend. He has served this department for thirty years and has finally put in for retirement—effective tomorrow. His loyalty is beyond question. He is really not leaving law enforcement completely, but has been recruited to the criminal investigation department of the United States Army. He will serve as a Lieutenant Colonel in that capacity. This officer really needs no introduction because he is none other than our Chief of Detectives, John Miller."

Miller stood up and thanked the Chief and read from a prepared speech, which took about twenty minutes.

O'Malley was very taken aback by Miller's retirement, as they had worked together well for numerous years. He felt a loss at Miller's leaving the department.

Miller, at the conclusion of his speech, looked at O'Malley and smiled.

The Chief then stood and stated, "Chief of Detectives Miller and I, as well as the Police Commissioners and the Governor, have chosen who will be our next Chief of Detectives of this Department. Almost everyone in the city knows his name and reputation for honesty and management. He is college educated, a total instructor in law enforcement, and he is the head of the Homicide Unit of our department. The Chief then motioned for O'Malley.

O'Malley rose from his chair and walked to the head of the table where the Chief waited. The Chief stated to Captain O'Malley, "Congratulations, James, you are promoted to the rank of Major. I also appoint you the new Chief of Detectives effective tomorrow at 0600 hours. You will receive your badge, rank, and new assignment at the 9:00 a.m. press conference scheduled for tomorrow morning.

O'Malley gave a short thank you speech and received congratulations from all in attendance. Colonel Small pulled O'Malley to the side and stated, "James, you are gonna like this news also. This afternoon my men apprehended Peter Morgan getting off the train in Chicago, Illinois. He is now in our custody. I am sure he will have a lot of information to give us, and then we will charge him with being a spy and hopefully have the son-of-a-bitch executed."

"That is wonderful, Colonel. I think that's even better news than being promoted!"

Chapter Forty-two

The next day, O'Malley attended the press conference and accepted his promotion to the rank of Police Major and his new assignment as Chief of Detectives. The contention of the Police Department was that for once they had a Chief of Detectives who really knew the business of being a detective and would get things done and back cases cleared that in the past would not have had much attention.

That evening, O'Malley called a meeting in his office to discuss with his homicide detectives how he would run the department's detective units in the future. He also informed the homicide detectives of their new boss, Detective Sergeant Walker, as he was promoted to Detective Lieutenant and assigned as supervisor of the Homicide Unit.

Detective Phil Bonacursso has been promoted to Detective Sergeant and will remain in the Homicide Unit as the Operations Sergeant. Detective Joseph Ryan was promoted to the rank of Detective Sergeant and will be assigned to the Burglary Unit.

O'Malley thanked all of his detectives for their service and loyalty. He further told them he would have an open door policy and that he would do everything in his power to jail all of the wolves of this city.

Within the month of April, thirty per cent of the police department had either resigned or been fired. Some were being prosecuted for corruption, all due to the list obtained by O'Malley's detectives in the investigation of Captain O'Bryan's homicide. Two city politicians were arrested and indicted for corruption—thus O'Malley kept his promise to Jonas Carter, a confidential informant.

Cast of Characters

Officers

Captain James O'Malley—Captain in charge of an elite homicide squad

Detective Sergeant John Walker—Second in command of an elite homicide squad

Detective Phil Bonacursso—Up-and-coming star in detective field

Detective Joe Ryan—Veteran officer, rising in investigative world

Detective Robert Croix—New officer rising quickly in the ranks

John Miller—Chief of Detectives

James Patrick O'Bryan—Captain in Kansas City Police Department —Commander of Kansas City City Jail

*William Toler—New officer assigned to East Patrol Division
*Joseph Smith—Officer assigned to East Patrol Division—drunkard and slacker
*Both killed in police chase

Dr. James Dooley—Jackson County Coroner

William Stipa—Police reporter

Colonel Tom Small—Army Intelligence—Anti-Terrorist Division

Gangsters and Others

Jonas Carter—Black bar owner & O'Malley's Confidential Informant

Marcus Kaymark—German—mastermind of tattoo murders

John Lazia—North End crime family boss

Zino Torrio—Kansas City crime boss

*Phil Simone
*Anthony Gizzo
*Gus Bruno
*Sal DeMarko

*Stone-cold mob killers

German Spies

Peter Morgan—Nazi trained spy located in Kansas City

Paul Joseph Gobbels—German spy

Heinrick Himmler—Morgan's boss

Acknowledgments

All authors usually have numerous people that they want to thank for their involvement in the writing and publication of their novels. I am no exception and I want to thank Dixie Weers for all of her help and inspiration that has kept me motivated in writing this novel. Her advice and counsel concerning this story kept me on the right track to finish.

Special thanks to Rebecca Auriemma, attorney-at-law, for the use of her office space in writing this novel.

Also to Margaret for her encouragement and proofreading this novel. She never complained about the re-reading of this book.